D1433574

3

THICKER THAN WATER

Dylan Jones is an ophthalmic surgeon who was born in Ystalyfera in the Swansea Valley in 1955. He has been married for eleven years and has three young sons.

Thicker Than Water is his first novel and has been made into a BBC film starring Theresa Russell and Jonathan Pryce.

Further Titles from Dylan Jones

THICKER THAN WATER

Dylan Jones

_Au 8.3_
Jon

This first hardcover edition published in Great Britain 1997 by
SEVERN HOUSE PUBLISHERS LTD of
9–15 High Street, Sutton, Surrey SM1 1DF,
by arrangement with Arrow Books.

British Library Cataloguing in Publication Data

Jones, Dylan, 1955–
  Thicker than water
  1. English fiction – 20th century
  I. Title
  823.9′14 [F]

  ISBN 0-7278-5144-6

Typeset by Palimpsest Book Production Limited,
Polmont, Stirlingshire, Scotland.
Printed and bound in Great Britain by
Hartnolls Ltd, Bodmin, Cornwall.

To Rhys Albert, our absent friend.

Chapter One

'Sam, I've found a suite. It's oak. The chairs need a bit of work but the table is gorgeous. It's in a little shop in the vale, miles from anywhere. The man was ever so sweet. He gave me fifty pounds off because I was "expecting", ha, ha. See, it has its advantages. I'll tell you all later. Probably be about an hour. Love you.'

Sam Crawford listened to Jo's voice for what was probably the thousandth time. He waited for the high-pitched tone that signalled the end of the recorded message and punched the eject button on the Ford's cassette deck. The Sony C60 popped out with a tinny rattle and he removed it, putting it in his jacket pocket where he carried it, a constant companion to his keys. He was glad he had the tape. He supposed he was lucky to have it.

Lucky, he thought ironically, *yes, really lucky.*

In all their years together, they'd never taped one another's voices – why should they? It wasn't something you did. And a video camera was one of those things he had always meant to buy but hadn't quite got around to. But he'd found the excited message on the answerphone when he'd got home from the mortuary. He wondered, with a pang of self-doubt, if by now he would have forgotten what she sounded like had he not had the tape. Of the two copies he'd made, he carried one with him; the other copy and the original he'd put in his bank for safe keeping.

Twenty seconds of speech on sixty minutes of high-grained ferric oxide and a photograph of her looking

1

tanned and healthy taken on a flawless August day in the Greek Islands were the only reminders of her he carried. He looked and listened to them often, though lately the frequency had diminished a little. He knew that this was not altogether a bad thing. It was a sign of recovery. He laughed to himself. Recovery. You didn't recover from something like that, you merely coped with the pain until it was at a level tolerable enough to allow you to function again as a social being without breaking down at the slightest reminder. Sitting in the car, he looked at the luminous dial of the quartz clock on the dashboard. It was nearly nine p.m.

He felt hopelessly disorientated. He'd slept for twelve hours on the plane but in a journey of thirty-six it had not been enough and the clock in his brain was telling his body that it was four in the morning. Reason enough for the odd detached feeling his brain was favouring, wasn't it?

Then why the hell wasn't he inside and tucked up in bed? His bed, the one he hadn't seen for six months?

Good question. Excellent question. One that he didn't like the answer to.

How many miles was it he'd come, ten thousand? And now that he was here, he couldn't bloody well face the final few yards to his flat – *their* flat.

He knew it was pathetic. What did he think was waiting for him? But he knew the answer to that one.

Nothing. Sweet Fanny Adams. And that was probably the trouble. Once he walked in through the door, there would be no possibility that he would ever wake up from the nightmare and turn over to find her arm resting on his chest, her breathing steady, her face childlike in sleep.

Sitting in the car, he stared across the street at the scaffolding around the warehouse they were converting. He recognised the company whose logo fluttered on a flag jutting out near the top. The same company that had converted his building. He swung his head to remind

2

himself of what it would look like eventually, the brickwork cleaned and repointed, the windows freshly painted with new ironwork spiralling up.

They had both wanted to be near the water, responding to some inner urge that neither had understood. Something to do with their respective upbringings, his proximity to a lazy Welsh river and hers to the sea.

He sighed inwardly and put his hand on the car door. In a moment he was outside, breathing in the ocean's faintly foetid smell as it drifted across the moor towards him on the breeze.

It was a first-floor flat, up two flights. His key turned in the lock with surprising ease. The timed light of the shallow lobby kicked in immediately he pressed it and then, with a simple movement of his wrist on the handle, he was back inside. He flicked on the lights and they glowed into being, subdued, indirect, the way she had liked them. His eyes drifted across the familiar landscape of furniture, lingering here and there, his mind kaleidoscoping through a rush of forgotten memories as he drifted into the living room like a man sleepwalking. If he'd feared there would be nothing here, he had been totally wrong. The room was full of her, her plants, her furniture, her soul.

Now, centred in the room that had been the anchor of their partnership, objects he'd half-forgotten ever existed triggered explosive charges of emotion that threatened to overwhelm him.

A carved wooden love spoon hanging above a colonial rocking chair transmogrified into Jo's pained expression as she'd thanked the distant aunt who had thrust it upon her on their wedding day. He felt a smile warm his mind as he remembered her lame excuses for never throwing it away despite her threats. *'It has a certain kitsch appeal though, doesn't it, Sam?'* Her eyes laughing as she said it, knowing how thin the camouflage of her superstition really was.

3

He dragged his gaze away only to lock on to a posed photograph of the giggling Crawfords on an Alpine mountain complete with chocolate-box snow-capped peaks as a backdrop. Jo in anorak and gloves hanging on to his arm as she fought the hysterical laughter that had bubbled inside her at the inept attempts of the Swede Sam had coerced into taking their photograph.

In the empty flat, Sam suddenly sniffed the cold ozone of Tigne in December, and felt again the gut-wrenching anxiety that had accompanied their trip down the mountain only minutes after the snap was taken. Jo had been nervous. The French runs were more difficult than their Austrian equivalents of the year before.

'Take your time,' he yelled at her from two hundred yards down the piste. 'Try and get some rhythm going.'

He watched her begin, noting with pleasure how she was beginning to emerge from ungainliness into elegance as she let her natural balance rule the skis. The big German came into his field of vision late. Arms flailing, hopelessly out of control. He shouted at Jo and she turned, losing her balance but avoiding a head-on collision, receiving instead a glancing blow that set her spinning. He saw her pivot, saw her arm go out to break her fall, heard the crack of bone in the clear air . . .

Sam shook his head, trying to clear it of this negativity. He didn't want to remember Jo in pain. He found himself standing near to the hi-fi, his fingers straying to the power button, pressing it, hearing from within a gentle whirring before the room was filled with music. Her music – their music.

Acoustic Alchemy. Another of their mutual discoveries on a trip to the States. Mellow guitar riffs from real musicians.

It transported him and, as though it were the final trigger of an incantation, she was there in the room.

He saw her sitting on the sofa, one elegant knee crossed over the other, her foot dangling a shoe, the inevitable magazine in her hands. But as he walked towards her, the image shimmered and faded into nothingness.

He turned to the kitchen and saw the espresso machine sitting squatly on the worktop. A birthday present.

And instantly she was there, cooing with delight as she opened the parcel, playing imaginary maracas and shuffling her feet in samba rhythm as she came towards him.

Sam squeezed his eyes shut and when he opened them again, she was gone.

He turned abruptly and went back to the music. It was too much. Sensory overload.

He pressed the power button and in the silence that followed he stood at the window looking out at the darkness beyond. And as he stood there, a new sensation came to him, a powerful sensation that was much more vivid than the mirages of before. Hairs prickled on his neck.

Someone was behind him, watching him, he was certain of it. And then he heard the voice.

'The door was open, Sam.'

A familiar voice. Familiar and yet in Sam's stretched and straining mind serving only to double his confusion.

He swung round. A figure stood silhouetted against the bright lobby light. It seemed to fill the doorway. A dark human form, large and oddly shapeless, not a female form, not in any way resembling her. Still Sam found his mouth shaping her name.

As if beckoned, the figure stepped into the room and Sam's terror-stricken face relaxed into a relieved grin.

'Hello, Paul.'

Paul came forward and grasped one of Sam's hands, pulling him into an embrace before standing back and surveying him.

'Jesus Christ on a bike. That isn't a Barry Island tan.'

Sam shrugged. 'You're looking pretty sharp yourself.'

'Lying bastard. I feel like a dog's bum and probably

5

look it. I'm working bloody nights this week. Drunks and aggravated assaults. Pain in the bloody arse. I'll be knackered by Saturday.' The Cardiff drawl had not diminished.

'How's Debbie?'

Some unnameable emotion crossed Paul's big, drawn face, but he suppressed whatever it was and said cheerfully, 'Orders are to take you back for a drink, if you're up to it?'

Sam wasn't, but the emotional charge that hung in the flat like the heavy air of a summer storm still buzzed at his head and an opportunity to escape it suddenly seemed welcome. 'Lead on,' he said.

He followed Paul's large overcoated frame downstairs, oddly comforted by his brother-in-law's brash intrusion. It was consistent with the Paul of old. Sam had often wondered what vocation his brother-in-law might possibly take up if the police force ever found a reason to dispense with his services. He had never come up with an answer. It was only too conceivable how Paul must modify his sometimes overbearing *bonhomie* into a more intimidating belligerence. Something Sam appreciated was essential in order to survive in Paul's work. Sam, in fact, had nothing but admiration for Paul's Teflon-coated ability to function in the city's underbelly and emerge apparently unscathed.

Downstairs was a car with its engine running and someone smoking in the driver's seat. Paul stepped across and spoke through a wound-down window before stepping back and waving the car off. Turning to Sam, he said: 'We'll take your car, all right? Gav'll pick me up in three-quarters of an hour.'

Sam nodded. 'You won't be missed then?'

Paul proffered a boyish grin. 'Gav's a good lad. He'll cover me.'

They talked of Sam's flight on the way over, but Sam couldn't rid himself of the feeling that Paul was a volcano about to erupt with some burning, suppressed anxiety. It

6

was as if he knew some awful secret he was sworn not to talk about. But, in truth, Sam was glad of the small talk. It meant that Paul wouldn't notice the tremor in his hand.

This is crazy, he said to himself, but it didn't help the tremor.

He hadn't seen Debbie or Paul for six months, not since he'd decided on his self-enforced exile. For two agonising weeks after it happened he'd tried to carry on regardless, in a futile attempt at diverting himself from the need to admit that his life was shattered. Looking back, it had been a bloody stupid thing to do, but he hadn't been very rational at the time. He'd even taken himself back to work, and that had been excruciating. Everyone had been unfailingly kind and sympathetic, but it was the last thing he'd wanted. What he'd wanted was to forget. For everyone to treat him like they had before the accident, as if nothing had happened.

People's kindness had almost destroyed him during those few, agonising days. So much so that one grey morning fifteen days after Jo's death, he'd bought a one-way seat on a Quantas flight and left the city and the friends and the memories in search of somewhere to let his wounds heal. And it was time rather than any specific place that proved remedial, although it was more palliation than total cure. After six months enough of the pain had eased to allow him to contemplate returning. It was the wisdom of that decision that plagued him now as he followed Paul through the door of their semi.

'Deb,' Paul yelled, working himself out of his overcoat. 'It's Sam.'

There was a noise from upstairs and Sam looked up and over his shoulder, hearing his breath lock in his throat. For a moment he wondered if his heart had actually stopped. He couldn't speak, he couldn't turn his head or blink his eyes for fear of shattering the illusion. His dead wife was walking down the stairs towards him.

7

It was Jo in every detail, Jo's long legs in a modest skirt, Jo's hands on the banister (was there a suggestion of her needing to steady herself?), Jo's face, Jo's Celtic blue eyes, and yet . . . And yet, was the face a little longer? Wasn't the mouth a little wider, the hair a touch darker? And then she was in the hall and coming towards him, two spots of high colour on her pale face.

'Oh Sam,' she said in a shaky voice as she embraced him. He held her and she even felt like Jo, but the voice had broken the spell. Of all things, the voice was different. He held her for a moment and then pulled back and looked at his wife's twin sister.

'Hello, Deb,' he said, and was surprised at how even his voice sounded.

'Oh Sam,' repeated Debbie quiveringly, 'I'm so glad you're back.'

'I'm glad to be back.' Out of the corner of his eye Sam saw Paul nodding slightly, as if in approval of a word or action. Well it was tough for all three of them, he guessed.

'Come in and sit down,' said Paul jovially and led the way through to the living room. A strong feeling of *déjà vu* struck Sam immediately he walked through the door. It took him a moment to understand why and then he realised that it had been redecorated since he was last there. Debbie had made it into an exact copy of his and Jo's living room as was. Same material covering the chairs and sofa, same curtains, identical pine table, same limited-edition print on the wall. Debbie, seeing his reaction, said simply:

'I bought it all two months after the accident. It wasn't until all the furniture was in place and the curtains were up that I realised what I'd done. Typically, Paul didn't notice anything strange about it. I'm sorry if it shocked you, Sam.'

He smiled reassuringly. Some people might have found it unhealthy, but not Sam. 'Bit of a surprise, that's all,' he said laconically, knowing that it should not have

8

been. He looked at the print. Its presence in the room symbolised Debbie and Jo's inexplicable relationship. It was a seascape, a moody depiction of some obscure, windswept Welsh inlet which they'd bought from different galleries as surprise birthday presents one year. They'd presented one another with similarly wrapped parcels and Sam had known even before they'd opened them to grins of mutual delight what they'd find. It was a classic example of the bizarre coincidences, for want of a better word, that had peppered their lives. Even now he hesitated at calling it anything as strong as ESP, although that, essentially, was what it came down to. Their empathy had echoed itself daily in their seemingly unwitting actions, as well as in the broader pattern that had shaped their lives. They had both gone to university in London, Jo to LSE and Debbie – mercifully – to Goldsmith's.

The one thing that had separated them at school had been Jo's undoubtedly superior academic ability. An ability that Jo, with admirable fidelity, always felt had been latent in Debbie too. Nevertheless, Debbie's application to LSE had not met with an offer of a place. Neither of them had ever considered their desire to be there at the same time as anything but natural. Its eccentricity was an outsider's perception. Just what mayhem their presence in the same establishment might have caused, Sam was left to imagine. As it was, London seemed too small for them. Socially they remained inseparable.

Sam had met them both at a party. They caused a stir wherever they went, their striking beauty somehow enhanced by its duplication. It was Debbie he'd been attracted to at first. She'd been slightly drunk, with a flirtatious streak and the louder laugh, but it was Jo's personality he fell in love with.

Months later, when Debbie had met Paul and they made up foursomes, the men would be astounded to see the girls turn up independently in the same dress with a

9

frequency that was beyond coincidence. Initially, both he and Paul had suspected collusion in the form of a sneaked phone call or even a rota system for the clothes, but their suspicions were unfounded. There was something the girls shared that singlets, as Jo used to refer to everyone bar her and Debbie when discussing the subject, didn't. Some subconscious understanding that their genetic cloning had unlocked. Paul, being Paul, had dealt with it in the same way as a lot of people did when confronted with something they could not understand – with complete derision. But thought concurrence wasn't that uncommon in twins, or so Sam had read. It seemed a real enough entity for worthy academic institutions to invest time and money in its investigation. It *was* weird, but in a nice kind of way. Something halfway between raining frogs and Macbeth's witches was how Sam teasingly liked to describe it to other people. 'A real Arthur C. Clark job,' he would say, smiling.

'Sam, are you all right?' asked Debbie.

He looked up, refocusing. 'Sorry,' he apologised. 'Lost myself for a minute there. The print,' he explained, pointing to it.

'I love that.' She paused before adding, 'So did Jo.'

Sam nodded. Paul came back in with two large pint mugs full of flat-looking beer. 'Home-brew,' he proclaimed proudly.

Sam took a sip and managed to hide his grimace behind a feigned smile of delight. It was tepid, almost unpalatably bitter and not in the slightest like the ice-cold Australian beer he had grown used to.

'Great,' he said.

Paul smiled broadly and took a large swallow of the beverage before asking, 'So what's it like to be back? How's the flat?'

'Pretty strange,' he said, answering the first question and surprising himself with his choice of words.

'Must be,' agreed Paul. 'Can't be all that easy for you.'

10

'I daresay I'll get used to it,' he said and earnestly hoped he would. He'd forgotten how grey everything was. Grey sky, grey houses, grey rivers, grey sea . . . grey people. He pinched himself mentally.

Come on Sammy boy, give it a chance.

He made an effort and showed them both pictures of his sister and her two great kids basking in the warm sunshine of Adelaide ten thousand miles away. He listened to Paul's account of his new role as a DC. It was a typically self-congratulatory anecdote, but Sam didn't mind because it meant that he didn't have to look at Debbie. He kept his eyes away. Looking at her was like stabbing himself with a rusty barb.

Seeing her, being in her presence, was worse if anything than the flat, which itself was an emotional whirlpool. Outside, a car horn sounded.

Paul looked at his watch, cursed, stood up abruptly and finished his beer in a couple of swallows.

'I have to go folks. Sam, I'll be seeing you. Any time you want to talk, or feel like a couple of pints, you know where I am.'

Sam nodded gratefully, accepting the offer in the spirit with which it was intended.

Paul looked at Debbie, and his face suddenly became serious.

'Remember to tell Sam about your shakes. He is a bloody doctor after all.' He turned to Sam. 'They don't seem to be able to do anything. Our GP is bloody hopeless.'

'What's all this?' asked Sam, knowing full well that Embridge, Debbie and Paul's GP, was more than competent.

'Oh Paul,' said Debbie tersely. 'Don't bother Sam with all that now. He's only just arrived back in the country, for goodness' sake.'

Paul sighed and said, 'Make her tell you, Sam, will you?'

'Sure, of course,' said Sam, bemused.

11

The corners of Paul's mouth turned up appreciatively and in an instant he was off. After he'd left and before Debbie came back in to the living room from seeing Paul off with a dutiful peck on the cheek, Sam had a sudden, inexplicable urge to leave too. The uncomfortable feeling he'd had ever since walking through the door rolled over in his gut like some large undigested snail. Debbie's letters to him in Australia, laden with just the right amount of angst, had ensured that Sam was aware of her need to keep their relationship alive. As much as Sam might have desired an opportunity to try to come to terms with what had happened and accept that it might entail confronting and then distancing himself from constant reminders, this was not, he feared, Debbie's perception.

He had tried to prepare himself mentally for meeting her, but the thought of being alone in her presence without Paul as a buffer brought back all the acute, aching yearning for Jo that had torn at him in the early days.

To his unmitigated distress, he realised that he was feeling desire for a woman for the first time since Jo's death. Feelings he had almost totally suppressed. Feelings that made him feel uncomfortable and somehow unclean. He had been prepared for a haunting, but this desire for the ghost was something he had not anticipated.

He looked at his beer and yearned for a Toohey's just as Debbie came back in looking oddly relieved.

'What was all that about?' he asked.

Debbie's eyes rolled up momentarily in an unmistakable look as she said, 'Paul can be a real old woman sometimes.'

'Well you do look tired. You both do.'

'Compared to you we look like troglodytes.'

'Seriously,' said Sam.

Debbie sighed. 'It's called myalgic encephalomyelitis – post viral fatigue syndrome in women's magazine language.'

12

'M.E.?' asked Sam, shocked.

She nodded. 'I had a flu thing the month you left. Since then I've been like a wet dishcloth. Some days I'm fine, like today. Others I shake, my legs turn to jelly and my brain to porridge. I get exhausted walking to the toilet. On those very bad days, I stay in bed.'

'You mean you've been like this for six months?' Sam asked, horrified.

Debbie nodded.

'But why didn't you tell me?'

'What could you have done?' she asked.

Sam frowned, caught off guard by her question. 'I don't know exactly.'

'Nobody does, exactly.'

'But you didn't say anything in your letters about being ill.' He'd found the veiled suggestions of her correspondence both enigmatic and discomforting, but unusually for Debbie, not particularly histrionic. He'd supposed it to be some sort of emotional problem. He hadn't suspected for one moment that it could have been physical.

'It's not the M.E. that's bothering me, Sam,' said Debbie, sensing Sam's thought. 'It's not why I wrote the letter.'

'Then –'

She interrupted him. 'Why do you think I asked you to come at this time, instead of for supper?'

'Your favourite programme on TV?'

She shook her head. 'You know damn well it was because Paul would be leaving at ten. I couldn't talk with Paul here.'

Sam felt the snail turn over in his gut again. It triggered a wave of nausea. He looked at his palms. They were beaded with damp droplets. He felt caged by Debbie's insistent gaze. He wanted to be a thousand miles away, and yet there was something in Debbie's words that commanded him to listen.

She said, 'I'm sorry about the intrigue, it's just that

13

. . . he'd be livid if he knew what I wanted to talk about.'

Sam frowned and wiped his palms on his knees.

'I tried talking to Paul, but he won't listen. He tries to be reassuring. He says it's just the shock of what happened to Jo. He's trying to be kind, but I know he thinks it's unhinged me somehow.' She paused, her eyes shining brightly. 'But I'm not mad, Sam.'

Sam's eyes narrowed. He sat back in the chair, cupping his chin in the palm of his right hand, his elbow resting on his left forearm, waiting.

'It started when I was first ill,' she began. 'The flu thing knocked me for six. It was then that I first had the flashes – that's the only way I can describe them. Like those adverts that are supposed to be illegal – subliminal programming or whatever it's called. They flash up for half a second and you're never quite sure what you've seen, but the next day you find yourself buying Zippo soap because they've stuck it in subconsciously. Well, this was the same type of thing.'

Sam studied her impassive face. Was there something in her eyes? An overbrightness? The burning undercurrent of the zealot or the plague sufferer?

'Did you have a fever?' he asked suddenly, managing to keep his tone even.

Debbie laughed mirthlessly. 'That's what Paul said. And the answer is no, I didn't. I wasn't hallucinating, Sam. And anyway, I don't have a fever now, do I?'

Sam paused. 'You mean it's still happening?' he heard himself ask.

Debbie hesitated, but her bright eyes never left his face. 'Yes, it's still happening.' There was something in her tone that suddenly made Sam wish he'd left when he'd had the urge to. This was exactly the sort of thing he'd been dreading. He suppressed a desire to jump up out of his chair and walk out, away from Debbie, away from a house that was a shrine to Jo's memory. But he couldn't. There was something almost sickeningly fascinating in what Debbie was saying.

'When Jo died,' she went on, 'it was as if something died inside me too. I can't explain it any better than that. Jo was always here.' She tapped her temple with the middle finger of her left hand. 'Like a faint buzz – a bit like the hum of a record deck that's switched on. Only no one else could hear it, of course, only me. When she died, it was as if someone had switched off the power.'

Sam nodded. He didn't understand it, but he knew what she meant. Jo had tried explaining it to him once. But her description was of a balloon inside her head that got bigger and smaller whenever Debbie was in trouble or needed her in any way. He remembered jokingly asking if he should arrange a brain scan for her.

Debbie had paused, allowing Sam to assimilate this information before she continued in a quiet voice. 'Lately,' she said, 'it's as if someone has turned the power back on.'

'What?' said Sam, his voice sounding croaky and dry.

Debbie nodded. 'The buzz is back.'

Sam swallowed and the sound of his parched epiglottis closing seemed incredibly loud in his ears.

Oh shit, no, he thought to himself. *No, no, no, not this, please, not this.*

A few days after it had happened, some well-meaning idiot had actually said to him, 'You'll get over it.' He remembered suppressing the urge to smash out at the sympathetic face. How anyone could have been so bloody insensitive, he would never know. But in fact, some time during the last month, in the sunshine of Australia and in the company of his understanding sister and unbiased strangers who hadn't known Jo and hence didn't look at him with the embarrassed, slightly uncomfortable expressions of those who had, he had begun to feel as if he was 'getting over it'. But this stuff! As if seeing Debbie was not enough, listening to her was twice as bad. He felt the sweat break out on his neck. A cold, clammy sweat.

'Jo's unhappy, Sam,' said Debbie, jolting him out of his mental roundabout ride.

'Jo's dead, Debbie,' he said pleadingly.

'She's unhappy, Sam,' continued Debbie as if she hadn't heard him. There was an absolute conviction in her voice that made Sam's contradictions seem unjustified and baseless. 'I know how it sounds. But I can't help it. She's unhappy. She's trying to tell me why. I don't know why yet, but now that you're back –'

Getting over it, said the voice in Sam's head. 'Jesus Christ, Debbie,' he said angrily, getting up from his chair.

'Sam, Sam. I know how hard this must be for you. It's been hard for me too. But I'm absolutely certain. You must trust me, Sam.'

'No!' yelled Sam. He swung away and brought his hand down with a cracking slap on the pine table, sending petals tumbling from some chrysanthemums in a blue-patterned vase. The pain in his hand and the noise jerked him into a sudden awareness of his reaction and when he turned to look at Debbie again, the expression on his face had changed to one of concern. 'Debbie, you know that what you're saying can't be true – you must see that.'

Debbie's smile was unshakeable. 'Oh, I know exactly what it sounds like. It sounds like Jo's little sister's mind has gone on a trip round the Crab nebula. Insight into the problem – how about that Sam, eh? That means it's not a psychosis, doesn't it?' She paused, leaning forward in her chair. 'I can't help how it seems to you, Sam. I only know it's happening to me.'

'M.E. can do funny things, Deb,' said Sam, knowing he sounded patronising.

'OK, Sam, OK. I didn't really expect you to react in any other way. I'll wait. I'll wait until you find out for yourself.'

Sam's brow furrowed, but all he could see when he looked at Debbie was her knowing, patient smile. He realised with disquiet that it was the very nature of this smile that bothered him so. It was simply so unlike

16

Debbie. Her affectations had plagued Jo's existence for years. Her demanding moods, her hypochondria. Had Jo's death affected her so much? Had it been the jolt she'd needed? They were unanswerable questions, and having no answers did little to assuage Sam's vexation. They didn't talk about it after that. Debbie, having broached the subject, seemed content to let the seed of doubt she'd planted germinate in Sam's brain. They talked about family and Paul's job and her illness and about the future. Throughout it all, Sam watched her eyes. The bright knowledge of what she had said earlier burned there with total conviction, at odds with her impassive features.

By eleven, Debbie had brought out canapés which he had been unable to face and his apologies for the increasing frequency of his feigned yawns met with sympathetic noises.

'Bloody jet lag,' was all he managed. She didn't object when he excused himself.

'Anything I can do?' she asked.

He shook his head. She and Paul had looked after the flat and it had looked scrubbed and glistening in the short time he'd been there. He left with a promise that he would speak to Embridge about her M.E.

Debbie thanked him, but there was scepticism written all over her face. 'I won't tell you not to bother, because Paul will expect it, but we both know that there's nothing to be done. It will run its course and there's nothing anyone can do about it. But thanks anyway, and thanks for coming over. Thanks for listening.'

'Debbie, I –'

'No, Sam. Don't say anything. All I ask is that you don't talk about this to Paul. He gets so annoyed. Please?'

'Of course,' said Sam without hesitation. 'I'll look in later in the week, see how you are.'

Debbie smiled appreciatively, but there was concern in her eyes. 'You look all in. Promise me one thing, Sam. Promise you'll look after yourself.'

Sam laughed. 'Me? I'll be fine. Next time I see you, I'll be back on the planet, honestly.'

'Perhaps by then we'll understand each other a little better.' She smiled another of her secret smiles.

The urge to scoff welled up inside him like a sneeze, but he bit it back. He suddenly felt very, very tired. He turned from the door and started walking towards his car. He'd gone a couple of steps when he felt something cold and wet on his face. He looked up and felt the beginning of a drizzle kiss his cheeks.

Welcome home, Sammy.

Chapter Two

He drove back to the flat numb and exhausted. His mind was a mush of confused emotions and several times he found himself inexplicably on the verge of tears. By the time he pulled up outside the flat he knew that he could not face a night there. Not now, not yet.

Without hesitation, he turned the car around and headed back to the city.

The Holiday Inn was heaving with partygoers, most of them drunk and full of alcohol-induced conviviality. A man in a dinner jacket wearing tinsel and a clown's hat was being helped into the lift as Sam approached the reception.

There was one girl on the desk. The plastic smile she flashed Sam belied the boredom and dark night-shift rings under her eyes.

'A room please?'

Her eyebrows arched dubiously as she started tapping instructions into a VDU in front of her.

'We have one left,' she said, still with her eyes on the screen, 'but it's a double?'

Sam shrugged acquiescently.

'Just the one night?'

'Just tonight.'

She gave him registration forms and waited for him to fill them in. Whilst he wrote, Sam asked, 'What's all the fuss?' as yet more revellers passed through the lobby.

The girl eyed him oddly before answering drily, 'Just the usual.'

Sam stopped writing and looked up. 'The usual?'

'Yes, you know. New Year's Eve.'

All Sam could do was shake his head in disbelief. He'd forgotten.

'I've just come off a plane from Adelaide,' he said wanly. The girl smiled sympathetically and ran his credit card through a machine.

'Then you won't be joining in the fun tonight, sir?'

Sam didn't answer. He merely took his key and walked towards the lift.

The room was stifling. In a daze, Sam threw off his coat and lay on the bed. Physically, his body cried out for sleep, but his brain stayed buzzingly in breakfast mode.

He switched on the TV. Its blue light flickered over his face. He punched through the channels disinterestedly, discarding a car chase – maniacal studio laughter and Clive James as dry as a bone.

Almost everywhere, people were celebrating, welcoming in the New Year, saying goodbye to the old.

Sam didn't want to think about the past year and found himself hardly able to contemplate the one to come.

Six days ago it had all seemed so plausible. Christmas dinner on the beach with his sister and her family. The sun had shone, they'd swum, eaten drumsticks and Christmas pudding with lots of ice cream, though still his sister had harboured those doubts he could see in her eyes.

So he had managed a locum for three weeks, so he hadn't lost his touch. So friggin' what, she had said.

He had only been away six months, she had insisted. The precious practice would survive without him for a few months more.

She didn't think he was ready.

Daniel, her youngest, had sat on his knee the day he'd told them he was going back. He'd cried.

'Don't cry, Dan,' his mother had said.

'I don't want Uncle Sam to go back to Wales. There are monsters and ghosts in Wales. Uncle Sam said so.'

Sam had laughed and cradled the child. 'Only stories, Dan. Just stories. No monsters or ghosts, honest.'

But the child was inconsolable and when he'd looked up to his sister for support, she had held his gaze and remained dumb. He had read a question in that penetrating gaze. One that asked, *Are you sure, Sam. Are you really sure?*

In the hotel room, Sam squeezed his eyes shut and tried to sleep. Tomorrow he would start afresh.

Tomorrow.

Two hours later, Sam stood at the window of his hotel room staring out at the unfamiliar view as rain spattered against the glass. He'd dozed for an hour and awoken with a start, disoriented and with his throat burning. Below, street lights shimmered and sparkled in the trickles of dark water that ran down the window. Gusts whistled over the city and the ropes from renovation work on the Railway Hotel rattled and clattered against the iron fire escape, frenetic percussionists in the elemental overture. A taxi, its light yellow and clearly illuminated, moved slowly along the street beneath. Sam wondered vaguely if they got paid extra money for working on a night like this.

A night like what, Sam? There's an average south-westerly blowing, that's all. They're used to it. This is bloody Cardiff, remember?

He took a sip of the Rémy he'd poured himself from the room's bar and felt the warmth spreading down his throat. He'd been standing at the window for twenty minutes, letting his eyes wander, allowing his mind the freedom to pursue its own course.

For fifteen minutes that course had never strayed from Debbie. Meeting her again had unnerved him greatly. It wasn't that he lent any credence to her arcane ramblings about messages from Jo, it was just that he felt he could have done without hearing them. But then the more he thought about it, the more he realised that he would have been surprised if something like this hadn't happened. Debbie had always been the more immature of the two sisters, the more emotionally labile, the moodier, the more dependent and demanding. Jo knew it and had been exasperatingly understanding, inevitably exonerating her little sister. At first, Sam had found it irritating, but he soon realised that Debbie and Jo's relationship was something that even he, as Jo's husband, could only impinge upon to a limited extent. If blood really was thicker than water, then their Celtic mixture had the viscosity of crude oil.

Over the last few years, Debbie's fragile ability to cope with the world at large had been stretched to its limits by her and Paul's unsuccessful efforts at having a baby. Sam, however, had not interfered, having long ago made it a rule to stay out of his own family's medical problems. It was not a good idea to have a sister- or brother-in-law on the books. Far better to let a colleague attend with the proper professional detachment. Which wasn't to say that Sam hadn't thrown in the odd helpful phonecall on their behalf, but there were only so many strings that could be pulled. With regard to Debbie and Paul's infertility problems, there simply weren't any more left to pull. Paul's sperm count was normal and as far as motility went, they were all bloody Mark Spitzes, as the lab attendant had so aptly put it. Debbie's hormone levels were good, she was ovulating regularly and her laparoscopy and dye had revealed no fallopian blockages. It was only a matter of time, they'd said. Two years of trying for the average couple, they'd said. But as eighteen months grew into twenty-four, and twenty-four into thirty, Debbie's anxiety and desperation had become increasingly evident. And although she never as much as once actually said it, it became obvious by her veiled hints and subtle remarks that she blamed Paul. Sam suddenly felt sorry for old Paul. Underneath the loud, exuberant, self-opinionated veneer was a man who could be hurt, who felt pain like any other.

And then Jo had fallen pregnant. The most ironic thing about it was that he and Jo hadn't even been trying. Of course, they hadn't been taking any precautions and they weren't stupid, but they hadn't been going at it hammer and tongs. Not like Debbie and Paul. Sam could still vividly remember the look of guilt and pain that had followed Jo's initial incredulous jubilation the day he'd brought back the test result and a huge bunch of flowers. He had known immediately what the problem was. Even at the moment of Jo's supreme happiness, she couldn't help but worry over how the news might affect Debbie. Sam had started to object to the wrist-wringing and was beginning to get exasperated when Jo's crumpled brows cleared and she announced, 'It's all right, I'll get Mary to tell Maude.'

The twins had been born as the only children of a respectable middle-class Welsh solicitor and his Irish wife, inheriting intelligence and deep blue eyes from the former, vivaciousness and flaming-red hair from the latter. From the outset, they had been totally independent of other children, content with their own company, speaking their own secret language. They fought each other's battles and had been fiercely loyal and sensitive to one another, as indeed they still were. Sam wasn't surprised by any of this. It was not uncommon twin behaviour.

At that first odd mention of Mary and Maude, Sam had stared at her bemusedly, and as if she'd just let out some desperate secret, Jo reddened and began giggling in embarrassment. Despite Sam's insistence on an explanation, it was only later and with much reluctance that Jo did explain. In so doing, she gave Sam a glimpse into the strange world that Jo and Debbie, as identical twins, had once inhabited.

On the occasions that she and her sister did argue, or when something unpleasant had to be done to one without the other, like visiting the dentist, or Jo's appendectomy, they had developed a defence mechanism to ward off the pain of the harsh words or separation. Their counteraction was to pretend that they weren't really sisters, but instead total strangers who could deliver and accept the bad news with the candour and indifference that total strangers might show.

They became Mary and Maude. No-holds-barred *doppelgängers* who were allowed to speak their minds in the knowledge that it would never jeopardise their true emotional stability. Sam had always felt like asking which of their 'states' exhibited the truest emotion, but he never had. It would have been oversimplifying things to take that road. And some things, oversimplified or not, were better left as they were. Especially since it was not information Jo volunteered terribly freely.

Jo had assured him that it had worked very well during periods of emotional stress for both of them, but that she hadn't even thought of Mary and Maude for years.

Sam knew better than to mock, for the same reason he hadn't mocked when Jo told him that she instinctively knew whenever Debbie was in trouble. There was simply another dimension to Jo and Debbie's relation-ship that he didn't understand, but didn't feel he had the right to dismiss. He'd let it pass, but the following evening, after Jo came back from visiting Debbie, he asked jokingly how Maude had taken it.

'Oh, Maude was a bitch and said I was far too old to think about children, but then she would,' she replied dimissively. And then a warm glow spread up over her face and she added, 'But Debbie was delighted. She cried her eyes out, poor love.'

The paradox of her reply was almost laughable, but he saw the relief in her eyes and accepted it as such. She had that way about her, a way of communicating emotion through her eyes. He sometimes wondered whether, had they been born a thousand years earlier into the Druidic culture of their ancestors, Jo and Debbie would have become priestesses. Perhaps they might even have been worshipped. Certainly they had the eyes for it.

Eyes that could tell you things, eyes that could bewitch.

Sam turned and walked across to his jacket, which he'd slung over the back of a chair. He found Jo's picture in his wallet and sat down to look at it. She was sitting on a wall, brown legs coiled beneath her, laughing as the warm Mediterranean wind ruffled her hair. He could almost smell the fresh bread from the small bakery on the village square and he knew that just after taking the snap, they'd walked around a corner to see a line of freshly caught squid hanging up to dry, tentacles waving in the breeze like pyjama cords.

'Jo,' he said wistfully, and then the mood passed and he grinned to himself. 'Look at me, talking to a ghost.' He smiled at the photograph. 'But if your crazy sister is right, I can expect a return call any minute.'

He imagined Jo sitting opposite him, giving him one of her special mock withering looks and saying, 'Don't hold your breath, Samuel.'

He stifled a giggle that was triggered by the image. *Not good, giggling to yourself. You should know better, Sammy boy.* But, like a flower in the sunshine, the giggle opened up into a laugh and when it finished, he felt the better for it.

He slept late the following day, ate a room-service, cholesterol-rich breakfast of eggs, bacon, fried bread and toast, and went back to the flat. It was a cheerless Tuesday, the road devoid of traffic on this New Year's holiday. He buried himself in unpacking, ran six miles around the docks and spent a couple of hours opening a small hill of accumulated mail. When night came, he uncorked a bottle of claret and drank almost all of it, quickly and without relish, adding alcohol to the jet lag that seemed truly worse on this second day after his return. The two combined to send him into deep oblivion, just as he had hoped they would.

The next morning was less of an ordeal than Sam had expected. He tried, in an attempt to get it all over with as quickly as possible, to see everyone who worked in the practice in the first half-hour. Everyone, with two notable exceptions, made an effort to react with the minimum of fuss, behaving as if he'd just returned from a fortnight's holiday. They enquired after his health with perhaps a little too much zeal, but otherwise were sensitive and kind. Sam reassured them all that he was fine and well, and remarkably enough, after an hour or so, it felt as if he had never been away.

The exceptions to the welcome normality of people's reactions came from two very different sources. The first occurred at nine o'clock that morning as Sam walked into the single-storey red-brick building that was the Victoria Road surgery. It was relatively new and the architect had leaned heavily towards natural light, creating a faintly Scandinavian flavour with a domed glass and wooden roof over the central reception area that alleviated the somewhat austere-looking exterior.

On his way in, Sam glanced at the brass plate to the side of the entrance, as if to reassure himself that he was still a part of it. His name was there, second on the list of four, underneath Jack Rioch's and above Peta Manton's and Ned Whelan's. As he pushed open the door, he saw Brenda look up from the reception desk, saw her complexion turn to ivory, her jaw drop and her face dissolve into tears.

Brenda was the backbone of the place. It was Brenda who knew every patient by sight, Brenda who made sure the coffee was hot and Brenda who baby-sat Peta Manton's kids and generally played mother to everyone remotely connected to the practice. She was loved and respected by doctors and patients alike. A rare achievement in a job where dragons still ruled unopposed in the majority of cases.

Sam hurried over to her and found himself, in the first minute of returning to work, reassuring and consoling someone over his own tragedy. After blowing her nose a few dozen times and sitting down, she'd recovered enough to sob, 'I'm sorry, Dr Sam, but seeing you walk through the door . . . it brought it all back. You must think me a silly old woman.'

Sam thought her nothing of the kind and said so, but found himself mentally praying that her reaction was not going to be typical. Thankfully, it wasn't.

Jack Rioch put his head around Sam's door while he was wading through the mountain of mail that had piled up. Sam took in the thumbs-up sign and the questioning arch of Rioch's eyebrows and nodded a grinning yes in answer.

'Any problems, my door is open,' said Rioch, who used words as if they were the rarest of gems, before vanishing like a rabbit down a hole. Five minutes later, Peta Manton walked in and kissed him on the cheek. She looked exactly the same as the day Sam had left. A capable mother of three with a penchant for dungarees and huge glasses, she was a favourite with the feminists in the practice, but Sam knew that, unlike most of them, she didn't take herself too seriously. He was very fond of her.

'We've missed you, Sam,' she said after the peck.

Sam nodded gratefully and asked, 'What news?'

'Nothing tabloidworthy, but I'll spill the available beans over coffee.'

Ned Whelan didn't call in on Sam. He didn't see Ned until coffee-time. Ned, God bless him, proved to be exception number two.

The small shoebox they all referred to as the coffee room had been completely redecorated since Sam had seen it last. The three anti-smoking posters had been removed and replaced with a Lowryish print bequeathed by a patient and a dubious landscape of some glowering hills. No one was quite sure if they were an improvement on the posters or not.

Peta was sitting reading the *Guardian* with a half-drunk cup of coffee when Sam walked in. She put down the newspaper and asked, 'How was it?'

'Surprisingly enough, Mr Agostini's backache is no

better, but his wife, I'm glad to say, is pregnant again. Mrs Albert's knees are much worse, except when she walks to the the Half-Moon twice a week, and . . . Need I go on?'

Peta grimaced. 'Welcome home.'

'Actually,' said Sam smiling, 'it's reassuring in a way to know that some things don't change.'

The door swung open and Ned Whelan breezed in.

He had joined the practice a year after Peta and eighteen months before Sam had. Neither of his junior partners had fathomed out what sort of aberration in Jack Rioch's normally rock-steady business acumen had allowed Ned to slip through the net. Rioch seemed to have accepted it as a mistake they simply had to live with and consoled himself with the knowledge that a favour owed to Ned's father, who had retired some years before from a lucrative and successful Harley Street O & G practice, had been paid back with interest.

Peta was less philosophical. She had confessed to Sam that the honeymoon period had lasted all of six months. That was how long it had taken Ned to realise that a busy general practice was not the road to fame and fortune he had thought it to be. His attitude had since degenerated commensurate to the expanding chip on his shoulder.

Ned felt that general practice was a mistake. To anyone foolish enough to listen, he would explain how he should have joined his father's practice had it not been for some debilitating illness robbing him of his opportunity during a crucial stage of his career. Whether or not he believed this himself was beside the point. What he did believe was that medicine existed for him to make money. Peta took every opportunity to point out that there was no reason why he shouldn't change tack even at this stage. Stranger things had happened at sea. Everyone knew it would be a hard slog: jobs with lousy hours, no social life for a few years, hitting the books, fellowship exams. In short, all the things Ned was allergic to.

Consequently, as his truculent behaviour alienated him to staff and patients alike, he entered a vicious spiral of unpopularity to which his response was more truculence and doing as little as his contract would allow.

He avoided Rioch with almost farcical skill. He disliked Peta because she spoke the truth to his face and enjoyed medicine for medicine's sake. He loathed Sam because he was good at it and the patients loved him.

Now, standing in the coffee room, he took one look at Sam, assimilating the tan and the trim frame instantly, and said, 'Well, well. The wanderer returns.'

Sam saw that there was a nervous smile on his lips and although the words were spoken lightly, the undercurrent of sarcasm shone through clearly.

'Hello, Ned,' said Sam affably as Ned walked over to the percolator and poured himself a coffee. He was a tall, swarthy man with dense wiry hair that always looked as if it needed cutting. Sam noticed he'd put on a few extra pounds while he'd been away and his jacket appeared well worn and slightly crumpled. 'How are things?'

Ned took a couple of gulps of coffee before replying and then said to the print above Sam's head, 'Busy. We've been carrying an extra load.' He paused before adding, 'As you know.' He looked at Sam then, a forced, challenging smile on his lips. Sam thought about saying something apologetic, but was prevented by Peta, who smiled sweetly and said:

'Actually, Sam, we've coped with your absence very well. It's been no worse than the four months of the year when one of us is away on holiday.'

Ned snorted. 'Perhaps some of us seem to have been doing a bit more coping than others.'

Peta turned on him sharply. 'That's bullshit, Ned. You know damn well that we've been absolutely scrupulous about sharing out Sam's patients.'

'Well all I know is that some of us never seem to have the time for cosy chats during half-hour coffee breaks.'

'And whose fault is that?' expostulated Peta, who was having none of it. 'If all of us started our clinics on time, there would be no problem, would there?'

Ned's face reddened darkly and Sam could see his jaw working silently. He watched in amazement as Ned slammed his cup down on the table, sending brown liquid up in a splaying arc that decorated the wall to a height of two feet, and stormed past Sam out of the room. He would have done better, it seemed to Sam, if he'd simply left without another word, but the temptation proved too much for him. He turned at the door and seethed, 'It's about bloody time, that's all I can say.'

'Ouch,' said Sam to Peta as he stared at Ned's back disappearing along the corridor at double time. As he watched he saw Ned stop dead in his tracks and turn to stare at one of the patients sitting waiting her turn. She had her back to Sam but there was something familiar about the incessantly joggling foot at the end of a crossed leg clad in vibrant floral leggings. As Ned stopped, so did the foot. But this halt in his retreat was only temporary. His back disappeared into his room and the door shut with a reverberating slam.

Sam turned to Peta, who tutted and dismissed the incident as she got up and poured them both another coffee.

'Sam,' she said. 'I'm sorry. He always was an insensitive bastard, but that was inexcusable. Our Ned', she sighed, 'has domestic problems.'

'Oh,' said Sam in a deep voice full of understanding.

'Hmm, thought it wouldn't surprise you.'

Sam shrugged.

'He still thinks he's the college stud. Now that he's realised he can't make money, he's decided that sex is the next best thing. Trouble is, he goes about it with all the subtlety of a rutting stag,' said Peta. 'I'm surprised his wife put up with it for so long.'

'Has Sophie actually left him?'

'Yup,' said Peta with obvious relish.

Sam found himself smiling at her reaction. 'I gather your sympathies are with her?'

'Ned's a big boy now. Time he learned to act like one.'

The remainder of the morning was remarkable for the ease with which Sam managed to slide into his old routine, enjoying the patient contact as he always had done and surprising himself into the bargain. But there was one other surprise awaiting him.

She was his last patient that morning, an addition to his list. She was also the girl in the corridor who had stopped Ned Whelan in his tracks, and as she entered he re-experienced the strong feeling he'd had when he first met her that she'd just unfurled herself from the masthead of a Viking longboat at the head of an icy fjord. A sunny blonde bob curled around to lick cheeks that curved flawlessly up into good, high bones. As before, it struck Sam that she had let her hair grow too long so that it hid her features when she hunched forwards, like half-drawn curtains. But there was no disguising the blue-green eyes that suggested the sea on a bright day, and she wore a pale colour on her full, down-curving lips. It was a face that might have been severe, even forbidding in its beauty. But the eyes wavered away from being held in any gaze, and the lips forever trembled on the brink of anxious concern. Neither lessened her striking appearance, but they rendered the mask imperfect. Above the leggings she hid herself in a voluminous, subtly patterned sweater that was easy on the eye, but which added to the overall effect of camouflage that permeated her appearance.

'Chloe?' he said with barely disguised surprise.

She smiled nervously and tried to find something to do with her hands. It was a characteristic gesture, one that Sam had seen and wondered about often, had commented upon on more than one occasion, only to be reprimanded gently by Jo's protective instincts.

They had met some eight months before Jo's death at

an exhibition of local artists. They had talked over wine and Jo had accepted an invitation to see some of Chloe's work that was not on display. That particular gallery didn't cater for still-life tapestries in rich sensual textures. Jo had taken an instant liking to the art and the artist. It had been a new departure for Jo, whose professional interest normally ranged from fine art to antiques. Indeed, it had been an unlikely pairing, but from their mutual interest had grown a firm friendship, which had been about to blossom into a business venture.

Sam had listened to Jo singing Chloe's praises often enough. On his own admission, art and design had never been one of Sam's interests, and he had merely made encouraging noises whilst Jo had enthused without really paying much attention to what they had had in mind. In financial terms it had not meant a huge sacrifice, and besides, Jo's money was her own. She had neither expected nor demanded that he get involved, for which he had been very grateful. The practice had been very busy setting up the necessary mechanisms for fund holding. It had taken up large chunks of Sam's time both at home and at work. Jo and Chloe met and planned in coffee-shops and tea-houses, but at weekends Jo and Sam made time for one another and he had never questioned the fact that Chloe never featured.

If he had wondered about it aloud, he only remember-ed hearing the word gooseberry muttered alongside assurances that Chloe was the sort who would simply hate to impinge. Now, confronted with her in the unexpected roles of doctor and patient, he realised that he knew very little about her. To an extent, he felt that blame, if blame were needed, rested with the two women. Chloe had been Jo's friend.

She had been working for a travel agent, he knew that. But he also remembered talk of the recession putting paid to it. It had been one of the triggers that had begun the business venture. It had always struck him as a little odd to think of her as a salesperson, although he hadn't said as much to Jo.

Sam had found Chloe a difficult person to talk to, swinging from reticence to an anxiety-induced verbosity, and he had harboured the feeling that she was uncomfortable around him. And yet Jo had voiced a genuine warmth and he had always trusted Jo's judgement, even if there had been a touch of the mother-hen about her protective attitude. That, he knew, was in the genes. He had never been able to take Jo within fifty miles of a dog's home for much the same reason.

And yet Sam had glimpsed in Chloe the odd touch of something that was at odds with the shrinking-violet image she portrayed. An occasional way of dressing, the odd uninhibited laugh that just didn't gel.

So what was it all about? Self-denial? He wasn't sure. But even as he mulled over all these fleeting thoughts, a blurred, uncomfortable recollection superimposed itself and sent a tingle down his spine. There was something else he should remember about Chloe, something important.

At his invitation she sat, crossing her legs and smoothing out the creases with long, compulsive fingers.

'Well . . . this is a surprise.'

She attempted a smile that hovered momentarily before lapsing into a sad parody.

'I had to come.' She spoke in distracted, broken phrases, her eyes flicking from his face to the calender on the wall with nystagmic frequency. 'After the funeral I . . . I couldn't bear . . .'

'That's understandable. It was a difficult time for all of us.' He saw tears spring to her eyes. She blinked them away, sniffing.

'I'm sorry. I didn't come here to bawl. I came to see Dr Manton earlier and then I saw that you were back. I hope you don't mind that I squeezed myself in.'

Sam watched her left hand. Devoid of rings, the middle finger traced an imaginary line up and down her leg in time to her joggling foot.

She sniffed again and took a deep breath, collecting herself. 'This isn't what was supposed to happen. I came to thank you . . .'

Sam wondered at the genuine tones tinged with bitterness. 'For what?'

Chloe laughed in a show of even white teeth. Once again Sam was aware of the transformation it produced. The laughing Chloe was an altogether different beast from the fidgeting worrier.

'You don't remember,' she said, and added half to herself, 'Why should you. I was probably the last patient you saw before . . .'

'Patient?' said Sam in confusion.

He turned over the pages of her records and found his own hand – just a couple of lines: *Smear positive. For urgent referral.*

And then he remembered. She'd looked different that afternoon. A pale shadow of how she was now. She had been worried, that was why she'd turned up. Worried because she hadn't had the result of the smear that had been taken a month before. Encouraged to overcome her reticence over abusing her social acquaintance of Sam by none other than Jo herself.

He looked again at the top corner of the front sheet of the notes and saw that the stamped initials N.W. had been crossed out and replaced by S.C. Of course. Now he remembered all of it. She had been Ned's patient, but Sam had agreed to see her, intrigued by her pleas. He'd been disturbed enough by her anxiety to search around for the result. A month was too long. Most smears were back within a couple of weeks. He'd gone into Ned's room and found the thing at the bottom of one of Ned's drawers. Just how it had got there, he hadn't a clue. He'd meant to talk to Ned about it. That sort of thing was sloppy. And what had been worse was that the bloody thing had been positive. He'd rushed a letter off to the hospital, and given Prentice a ring for good measure. It must have been the last thing he'd done that afternoon.

The last thing he'd done before going home and finding the policeman on his doorstep.

'I remember now,' he said finally.

'Six months of laser treatment and discharged last week,' she said.

'That's excellent news, Chloe.'

She didn't respond, her eyes riveted by the Swiss landscape on the calender.

'Everything's all right, isn't it?' probed Sam.

Her eyes fell to the elaborate flowers climbing her legs. 'I tried coming to the flat to speak to you, but I couldn't face it. Not there.'

The space between them filled with silence as Sam waited for her to say whatever it was that had really brought her.

'I spoke to her that morning, did you know that? It was me that sent her there.' Her eyes flicked up.

Sam held her gaze. 'To the antiques shop?'

Chloe shook her head. 'No. I'd sent her to look at some premises for us. They would have been ideal. The antiques place was a few doors down.'

'But she was happy with what she found there.'

'Happy?' Chloe tilted her head in disbelief.

Sam nodded. 'Happy. Despite everything that happened after that, she was happy at that moment. She phoned me. I know how she felt.'

'If I hadn't –'

'This will do you no good at all,' said Sam firmly. The sharpness of his tone stopped her. She looked away and nodded feebly.

Sam read Peta's entry in the notes from earlier in the morning. 'I see Peta wants you back in six months or so.'

Chloe smiled thinly.

'OK, let's keep this visit social.' He added in a softer voice, 'And if you want to talk, give me a ring.'

The thin smile got up with her and left.

After she'd gone, he turned back to his paperwork and by the time he'd waded through the remainder of the post, it was almost one. He needed to pick up some groceries before he started his afternoon rounds. He waved goodbye to Brenda and walked out into an almost deserted car park. He saw Ned Whelan pulling out into traffic, still driving his old open-topped Spitfire. He laughed to himself. The day had opened out and a weak sun filtered down through scudding brown clouds, but the breeze reminded him that it was January. It must have felt Arctic to Ned, but of course he would never have admitted it. He fumbled in his pocket for the unfamiliar keys – he'd rented the Ford at the airport, not knowing what state his own car would be in after six months parked outside Debbie's house. As it turned out, his worries had been groundless. Paul had started it regularly, but Sam had arranged for a service anyway, since he still had plenty of time left on the rental, which had come free with the flight.

He put the key in the lock. It slid off and his knuckles rapped painfully against the paintwork. He swore silently and tried again, this time leaning forward slightly to watch the insertion. It wouldn't go. He stared at the key. Yes, it was definitely the right one. The hire firm's logo gleamed garishly on the key-ring. After four more attempts at the driver's side, he shrugged and tried the passenger door. The same thing happened, and the boot showed precisely the same reluctance. The key just would not engage. It wouldn't even go in a quarter of an inch. He hadn't had this trouble before. It was definitely the right key, but was it the right car? He suddenly, fleetingly, felt very foolish. But no, damn it, there was his newspaper on the back seat, where he'd left it. He stared perplexedly at the car, shaking his head in disbelief.

'Having trouble?' asked a voice from behind him.

He swung around angrily but the curse died on his lips as he saw Chloe Jesson standing watching him.

'You still here?' she shrugged and rattled the Superdrug carrier bag she was carrying.

'Ran out of war-paint and toothpaste,' she explained

drily; 'it's not for me to say but isn't it a little cold to stand about admiring paintwork?'

'Locks are jammed,' he said concisely. He tried inserting the key three or four times to back up his story.

'Have they seized up in the cold?' she offered meekly.

'God alone knows.'

'Umm . . . can I give you a lift anywhere?'

He pondered the situation for a moment or two and then asked, 'Are you going into town?'

Chloe nodded.

'Right. Give me a minute to phone the hire company and I'll be with you.'

When he returned from explaining his predicament to a disinterested girl at the hire-car office, who nevertheless promised to get it seen to immediately, Chloe was already sitting in her car.

Sam was pleasantly surprised to see that she drove with confidence. He studied her surreptitiously. It felt strange to be in the car with her. Until this moment he'd always looked upon her as an accompaniment to Jo rather than a person in her own right, almost like a pair of bright earrings, pleasant but inanimate. It troubled him, both from the point of view of his previous blinkered state and because he seemed so aware of her now. She seemed much more relaxed in the car. More in control. He commented upon it.

'One of my vices. I love cars and driving.'

Her perfume filled the car. He'd forgotten what it was like to be in a car with a woman. Who needed air freshners? It had been like that with Jo. Whenever they'd gone out for the evening, he would get into the car the next morning to drive to work and he'd smell her perfume everywhere.

'So,' he said eventually. 'How's business?'

She smiled ruefully. 'What business?'

'I thought. . . ?'

'I didn't go ahead with it after Jo – '

'So what are you doing?'

'Temping for an insurance broker.'

'I see.'

She glanced across, amused by his response. 'It's not as bad as it sounds.'

They lapsed into silence again. Above the High Street, several forlorn-looking Father Christmases swayed in the breeze, pulled by ageing Rudolphs. The tinsel and aerosol snow of the shop windows served as gaudy remainders that Christmas had come and gone. It was an oddly depressing sight.

'How are you going to manage without a car?' asked Chloe as they pulled up outside an office block.

Sam shrugged. 'Taxi I expect. The rounds have to be done.'

'Why don't you take this,' she said and proceeded to shoot down his protests with insistent logic.

'I'm going to leave it in the car park all afternoon, anyway. Just another opportunity for it to be stolen or vandalised. You'll be doing me a favour.'

He finished his rounds by four. Shortly afterwards he drove into the surgery car park to find the door of his hired Ford open and a man in overalls sitting sideways in the driving seat, fiddling with the locks.

'What was the trouble?' asked Sam as he approached.

The mechanic, a glum-faced youth resplendent in torn and battered overalls, gave Sam a sour glance and said, 'Someone don't like you, mate.'

'No?' asked Sam innocently.

'I had to go back to the depot, didn't I. Don't carry the stuff in my van, do I.'

'Stuff?'

'Bloody superglue remover. Someone went and glued you up, mate. Rock bloody solid they were. I've left the passenger door and the boot. It's taken me all afternoon to get the bloody driver's side open.'

'Superglue?' said Sam incredulously. 'But who –'

'Like I said, mate, someone don't like you. Either that

38

or it was kids. Anyone else in the car park get glued?'

Sam shook his head uncertainly.

'Then as I said, mate, someone don't like you.' He stood up and gave the lock a couple of squirts from a can of lubricant. Then he slammed the door shut and opened it again with a smile of satisfaction. 'Thank Christ for that. It's a bugger to get out.'

Sam thanked him and gave him a fiver that transformed his glum face into a watermelon smile. He took Chloe's car back to her car park, left flowers on the passenger seat and put the keys in the exhaust pipe as arranged. He managed to get the mechanic to follow on and give him a lift back to the surgery so that he could pick up his own.

He drove home in a reflective mood with the mechanic's favourite phrase ringing in his ears.

'Like I said, mate, *someone* don't like you.'

Chapter Three

Sam knew there was something different about the flat the moment he walked through the door. The hall was barely larger than a big cupboard and had four doors leading off it, one to each of the two bedrooms on the right, one to the bathroom directly in front and one to the lounge/diner on the left. There was no natural light, illumination came from a single ceiling-mounted globe worked by a timer switch to the right of the front door. He stood in the hall, his senses straining to pinpoint the subtle change he'd noticed. What was it? A sound? No, everything was quiet and the hall looked just as it had that morning. So what? What was it? Without warning, he was suddenly plunged into a dense, inky blackness as the timer kicked off.

He heard his own breath hissing into his chest as he inhaled involuntarily. The darkness engulfed him in its totality. He was neither particularly claustrophobic nor scared of the dark, but the strangeness of his surroundings and the heightened pitch of his senses reacted at that moment to throw his mind down a tunnel of memory that had been sealed off for a long, long time.

At the end of the tunnel was a white door with a big silver handle. Terrible, muffled noises came from behind the door, and in the quiet of the darkness the noise became audible as a small, frightened, miserable voice full of desperation. Sam knew what was behind the door. He knew that it must have been dark inside the place the door guarded. Dark and cold and frightening.

He reached out wildly for the timer switch.

He saw his hand reaching out for the big silver handle on the white door at the end of the tunnel.

He groped behind him for the switch, sweat springing in cold, clammy beads on his back and neck.

His hand clasped the silver handle and pulled . . .

His finger scraped over the wall to the right of the switch.

He heard the white door give reluctantly with a sickly plop. It started to swing . . .

His hand brushed the switch . . .

. . . slowly, heavily open . . .

He jammed his palm inwards, his breath churning raggedly in his throat, feeling the switch glide in under the pressure and . . .

It was the smell that hit him first. A smell like a bad tin of dog food he'd opened once. But there was no dog food behind the white door. Dog food wouldn't try and get out . . .

Click! The light came on above him. It hummed with an electrical drone, like the buzz of honey bees in the . . .

. . . endless landscape of a summer a thousand years before. He had been nine, and the days had stretched before him like the blank pages of an unwritten book. His aunt and uncle had rented a cottage near to his family's summer retreat. Two miles was nothing to cycle on quiet lanes with the wind in your hair and your T-shirt around your waist when there were cousins waiting for you. His were tall Northerners from Humberside. Richard, who was Sam's age, and Alice, who was six, had the heart of a lion and the temperament of a crazed gorilla. Nothing was too high to climb or too wide to jump or too revolting to eat or too unbelievable to believe for Alice. Sam loved her, even though he didn't know what love was. They played endless games, Alice, not surprisingly, always insisting on being the cannibal chief, or the one-eyed pirate, or the headless ghost.

41

The three of them were inseparable that summer. With Sam's sister tagging along, it made four irrepressible musketeers untainted by the tribulations of being teenagers. Revelling in the true age of innocence and the magic of their inspired imaginations.

But forbidden fruit was always the sweetest. About a half a mile from where Sam lived stood a scrapyard. Half an acre of doorless cars, tin baths and a variety of flotsam that was a kid's dream of adventure. Who needed theme parks? They had had their own.

The yard was strictly off limits, but the owner had become an alcoholic recluse and the council had been meaning to clear the site for years. As a result, the musketeers had a free rein.

One hide-and-seek morning, bored with looking for and not finding Alice and Sam's sister, Sam and Richard had slid off to the village to watch a funfair being erected. Parental consent was obtained, the assumption being that Sam was the spokesman for all four.

Teatime was roll-call. Five p.m. sharp, the summer's one unbendable rule. That day, that particular warm, sunny day, only three apple-cheeked musketeers turned up. Sam's sister had assumed Alice had gone with the boys and Sam had assumed the opposite. Their oval-eyed bewilderment signalled the first seeds of unease.

By five-thirty, Alice's mother was very jittery, eyes glittering as she listened to Sam's father's confident reassurances with ever-increasing fear.

And Sam could only watch in bewilderment and not understand the odd queasy feeling in his stomach. By six, phone calls were being made and at seven the police were out searching, Sam in wide-eyed tow because he knew her haunts.

It was beginning to get dark when they got to the junkyard. It was there that Sam had the bright idea of looking in the space station. So called because there were five rusting cars arranged in a circle above a pile of other rubbish. Behind the space station was the fridge.

Sam remembered it as a huge white monstrosity with a massive silver handle and the manufacturer's logo broken off. Alice must have thought it a very clever place to hide, he had told his mother later, not seeing her horror at his calm, truthful explanation.

Hermetic rubber seals were still years away from Devon that summer. Instead, there were metal handles on the outside only. And there were public-information bulletins about abandoned fridges. Warnings never to go near them. Never ever to play inside one for fear that if the door slammed . . .

Even in the moonlight, her face was black. Swollen and silver-black. Her nails broken and bloody where she'd tried to claw her way out of that cold white metal tomb with no one anywhere near to hear her screams . . .

'Poor little Alice. Poor little Alice.'

He heard his mother's weary, troubled voice echoing, and leaned weakly against the timer switch, keeping his palm pressed flush against the housing. He left it there while he opened the lounge door and in one movement stepped inside and flicked on the light, shutting the door behind him. He stood with his back to it, shaking slightly as he studied his palm. There was a red ring of pressure there.

Christ! What the hell was going on? It was years since he'd had that particular nightmare, yet it had been as vivid as if it had happened yesterday.

He took some deep breaths and stared about him. The flat held so many memories and yet he had forgotten something as simple as the timer. He'd have to remember about that bloody light. God, that had shaken him. He took off his jacket and walked through into the bedroom. It was there that it struck him again, the different thing he'd noticed as he'd walked through the door. It was very strong in the bedroom, almost heady. It was a smell, an evocative, rich perfume. Jo's perfume – the one she always wore for him. He dropped his jacket on the floor in a daze and walked over to the bed. He'd made it up that morning before leaving for work, it was one of the rules he lived by. He knelt down. It was stronger there. He put his face close to the covers. It was a double bed; he preferred the space it offered and he'd never got used to singles again. He sniffed the bed, like a dog. It was strongest on the pillow, the one he didn't sleep on – *her* pillow. His mind reeled away from the realisation of what he was thinking. It couldn't be happening. Had he spilled some aftershave that morning? No, of course he hadn't, it was nothing like his bloody aftershave. It was perfume – very West Coast, very Jo.

He turned towards the dresser, yanked open the drawer. The bottles were all there, arranged neatly and he reached for one. It was simplistic in design, Aztec lines, half-full of yellowish liquid. He picked it up and red the label: Juanita.

He had come home late from work. It was summer, the windows in the front of the flat were open, but they kept the bedroom windows shut against the noise of traffic. She had a simple supper waiting and some chilled wine. There were birthday cards on the table.

His.

Thirty-three.

She had bought him some CDs and a shirt, complaining as usual that he had everything anyway. They lingered over the wine, not having to make much effort, comfortable in their own company.

He stacked the dishwasher while Jo changed. She'd bought something that morning and she wanted to try it on for him.

She called to him from the bedroom and he went in, unsuspecting.

She was on the bed, a thin sheet covering some of her, the most interesting part.

'Happy Birthday, Sam,' she said.

He laughed in delight, feeling himself instantly aroused, and stammered, 'What about this thing you bought?'
'I'm wearing it,' she said and pointed to her neck.
He stared bemused whilst Jo growled in frustration.
'Come here you big lug.'
He went to her and she offered her neck. Kneeling on the floor he smelled her.
Heady and musky, she knew what he liked.
'Mmmm . . .' he said as he kissed her. 'What is it?'
'It's called Juanita.'
He kissed her neck, pulling the sheet away with his free hand, letting his hands roam over her thighs and breasts.
'Juanita, Juanita, I wanna eat ya.'
Jo giggled deliciously and waited while he unzipped himself with difficulty. He was hard already.
Propping herself up on one elbow, she said, 'Me first.'
Reaching out with one long-fingered hand she grabbed him and pulled him towards her open mouth with its lizard-quick tongue . . .

He felt his heart's staccato beat in his chest. He got up suddenly and paced back and forth, leaving the room twice, only to come back into it again. After ten minutes and three hundred yards, he went back into the lounge, switched on the TV without the sound, poured himself a generous brandy and sat down. He stared blankly at the screen, trying to make some sense of what was happening.

Sam was a pragmatist and always had been. His only contact with psychiatry during his training had been a two-month attachment to a behavioural unit at Muswell Hill. There he'd come across obsessives and agoraphobic and behavioural disorders that had only left him confused. It hadn't been real medicine to him. He'd wanted to tell those pathetic people to pull themselves together. He'd realised that his response was unfair, but he'd been young and inexperienced and he'd tarred all

45

neuroses with the same brush. So he'd shied away from psychiatry as a Cinderella subject and he'd managed pretty well without it. The little he did know was that differentiating illusion from reality was the bedrock of sanity.

So where the hell did that leave him?

He took a slurp of the brandy and it stung his throat. He knew who he was, he knew where he was and he could remember all of what had happened that day. That meant he was orientated in time and space, and he didn't believe himself to be insane.

So what about the jitters in the hallway and the perfume, Doctor?

The jitters had been real enough, the memory of something that had actually happened, brought on by the darkness. But what of the perfume? Either he was imagining it, or it, too, was real. If it was real, then . . .

His mind flew to Debbie. Calm, confident Debbie with her knowing smile. She'd been so sure, so absolutely certain that Jo . . . Sam thumped the arm of the chair he was sitting in so violently that he heard wood crack. '*No!*' he said out loud. 'It isn't possible. Jo is *dead.*'

'*Jo's unhappy, Sam.*' He heard Debbie's voice in his head.

It wasn't possible.

'*The buzz is back, Sam.*'

Things like that just didn't happen.

'*I'll wait until you find out for yourself.*'

It couldn't be. It just couldn't be.

The knock on the door startled him so much that he spilled half the brandy over himself. He didn't get up immediately, wondering if it had been just his over-worked imagination. Then it came again, firmer, more insistent this time. He stood up and walked over to the door, hesitating as his hand reached for the knob. An image sprang to mind, an atrocious, despicable image of a bedraggled, decomposing Jo on the other side of the

46

door, her skin waxy and dirty, her mouth full of earth, her eyes lifeless but full of motion as things moved behind them. Too much *Twilight Zone*, he said to himself through gritted teeth, but his hand was moist as it closed on the brass knob and he had to wipe it on his trousers before he opened the door.

It was Paul. He took one look at Sam and said, 'Jesus H. What the hell happened to you?'

'I, uhh, spilled my drink,' said Sam clumsily.

'Are you sure?' persisted Paul. 'You look like you've seen a –'

'I'm fine, honestly,' interrupted Sam. 'Come in, for Pete's sake.'

He turned and walked through to the lounge and into the kitchen. 'I was just about to make some coffee,' he said over his shoulder.

'Great,' said Paul. 'I could do with one.'

Sam busied himself with the mundane, *sane* tasks of filling the kettle and spooning instant into cups. When he peeked out at Paul, he saw him staring at the prints on the walls or fingering the shelving inquisitively. Sam didn't interrupt and by the time the coffee was ready, he'd recovered himself and felt better, more in control.

'Must have been tough going back today?' asked Paul, spooning sugar into his cup.

'It had its moments,' replied Sam, glad of the let-out.

'I came to see how you were settling in.' Paul looked around admiringly. 'I love this place. Cracking view.'

'Yeah, cracking,' said Sam. 'I ought to have thanked you for looking after it.'

'Oh Kerist, Sam, no problem. Had a few of the uniformed boys drive around couple times a night. Enough to keep the bogeyman away. Oh, here, this is your spare key.' He removed a latchkey from a key-ring in the shape of a miniature truncheon and handed it to Sam. He carried his coffee over to stare out of the window at the cranes. 'They'll be building a bloody marina here next. I used to play here as a boy, used to

47

chase rats under these wharfs. Big grey buggers with tails as long as your arm. I expect they've all been gassed or neurotoxined by now. They're changing the city beyond recognition.' He sounded almost wistful.

Sam was silent, waiting for Paul to get to the real reason for his visit. It was uncharitable to think like that of Paul, and he was genuinely grateful for his efforts in minding the flat, but he knew him too well to suspect anything less.

Paul swung around, his big face creased and troubled. 'I'm worried about Debbie,' he said.

'Paul,' said Sam apologetically, 'I'm really sorry. I meant to ring your GP. I didn't get round to it.'

'No, it's all right. I'm bloody glad you didn't. I wanted to talk to you first. See what you thought.'

'Thought?'

Paul hesitated, as if he knew that what he was about to ask was pushing things a little too far. 'Last night, what did you and Debbie talk about?'

'Last night?' asked Sam, hedging. He'd promised Debbie that he wouldn't tell Paul about her bizarre convictions. 'Lots of things.' He knew it sounded hollow and he was dreading Paul's insistence.

'Did she talk about us?' asked Paul suddenly, as if he'd held the words in his throat all day and could keep them there no longer.

'What, you and Debbie?' said Sam.

'Oh, come on Sam, please. I want to know what she said to you. She doesn't talk to me any more. Did she say anything about us? About having a baby?'

Realisation hit Sam like cold rain. 'No, she didn't. Aren't things going well?'

Paul snorted and shut his eyes. 'No,' he said tiredly and flopped down into a chair. 'Things are not going well. We don't sleep together any more, Sam. We haven't done for months. Ever since Jo died, ever since this bloody M.E., we haven't even talked about kids. Before that, she . . . *we* were all for it. I haven't pushed it, obviously. I just thought that . . . last night she might have . . .'

Sam shook his head in reluctant denial.

Paul's frustration boiled over. 'Well what did you bloody talk about, for Christ's sake?'

'Paul, I . . .' mumbled Sam awkwardly. What the hell could he say to this man whose marriage was already under strain? *Weeeelll, we talked about communicating with the dead for a while, and your wife is convinced that her sister is about to emulate a certain Lazarus* . . . But as he watched for Paul to react to his reticence, Sam noticed his expression change from belligerence to one of trepidation.

'Sam, I know that Debbie has been waiting for you to come back. I know that she wrote to you. She hasn't said so, but I know she thinks you can help her.'

'With what, Paul?'

'If I knew that I wouldn't be here asking you.' Again, the anger showed through, but this time Sam interpreted it as frustrated concern.

'You're right, Paul.' He sighed acquiescently. 'She did write to me, and reading between the lines it did look as if she was having difficulty adjusting, but it hasn't been easy for any of us. Now I'll do what I can about the M.E., but until she tells me what else she thinks I can do, I'm as much in the dark as you are.'

He felt lousy lying to Paul, but he knew he didn't have any alternative. He'd given Debbie his word. A voice inside him said, *Take him into the bedroom and ask him if he can smell the perfume, Sam. Go on, do it!* And part of him wanted to. Part of him wanted to very badly.

But he couldn't. He was scared of Paul staring at him with that suspicious look of his, and laughing at the big joke. '*You had me going for a minute there, Sam. Jo's perfume? Ha, ha. All I can smell is yesterday's socks. Ha, ha, bloody ha.*'

'Promise me you'll talk to her, Sam,' entreated Paul.

'Of course I will.'

'I know what it must be like. Debbie and Jo were so close physically, it must be difficult, but –'

'It's all right, Paul. Really.'

That seemed to satisfy him. Sam offered him some brandy, but he declined it with an anxious glance at his watch. Sam watched as he shifted nervously in his chair, looking distinctly uncomfortable.

'You OK, Paul?'

Paul didn't answer immediately. Instead he looked down at the carpet, sighed and blurted out, 'Did you talk about Jo?'

'Of course we talked about Jo,' said Sam.

'Did she say anything about Phipps?'

'Phipps? Who is Phipps?'

Paul grimaced as Sam repeated the name, and then said apologetically, 'Look, Sam, I felt I ought to tell you before you hear about it from anyone else. There's nothing to it, we know that. The guy is a certified lunatic. If I had my way I'd shoot the lot of them and –'

'Paul,' said Sam calmly, interrupting the tirade, 'what the hell are you talking about?'

Paul paused and with a resigned sigh said, 'Two months after you went, a man called Phipps gave himself up and confessed to Jo's murder.'

'What?' breathed Sam incredulously.

'Sam,' said Paul entreatingly, 'I'm sorry even to have to mention it to you, because it was nothing, really. But if I don't tell you, you'll find out from someone and then you'll hate me for not having told you.'

'But why didn't you?'

'Because,' Paul said, 'Phipps is a crazy. The press, of course, had a bloody field day and it took us nearly a week to find it out, but we did in the end. And when I say crazy, I mean crazy. He's been in more strait-jackets than Houdini. And don't ask me why he did it, because only Phipps and the cuckoo know the answer to that one. Like I said, he should have been locked up a long time ago and that's all there is to it, *finito*.'

'But surely –'

'But surely shit, Sam. I'm mentioning it only so that it can be forgotten, OK?'

Sam stared at him in bewilderment, his mind a sudden whirlpool of doubts and questions.

'Jeesus,' said Paul when Sam's silence persisted. 'Do you think we would have let the bastard go if there was any possibility that he might have done it, eh? He can't even drive. Rode a clapped-out ten-speed Raleigh everywhere. You must have seen him around town?'

Sam shook his head reluctantly and Paul put his hand briefly on Sam's shoulder in a rare demonstrative gesture. He got up without another word, refilled Sam's glass and helped himself to a small one. He watched as Sam, wide-eyed, sipped the brandy.

'Sorry, Sam,' he said again, but Sam waved away his apology as unnecessary and only half-heard Paul excusing himself a few minutes later.

Sam spent the remainder of the evening trying to make some sense of the day's events. None of it was explicable, but the brandy made it all more acceptable. His desire to go back into the bedroom proved overwhelming and unhelpful. Juanita still lingered evocatively and having indulged himself for the fifth time, he felt the memories coming thick and fast, replaying themselves in front of him in glorious technicolor with the distorted detail of semi-hallucination.

He saw his hand reach out towards the stereo. Two pushes of his fingers and her sound was in the room. Old stuff that her father had played to her on crackling 78s, now brought to acoustic clarity by electronic wizardry that snuffed out the clicks and crackles and transferred it all on to pristine, indestructible CDs. Dorsey's trombone eased into 'Once in a While', flowing out into the room like chocolate milk.

Losing himself in the sound, Sam wandered into the kitchen and flicked on the light. The gleaming espresso machine glinted at him. He turned to the fridge, but as

51

his hand reached out for the handle, he heard little Alice speak to him from inside, like a malicious ventriloquist's dummy.

'*Look behind you, Sammy.*'

He pivoted and saw his wife at the sink, leering at him.

'*Ciao, baby.*'

Sam squeezed his eyes shut. When he opened them she was gone. He turned and ran into the living room, shutting off the noise with his finger and leaning weakly against the bookshelf. It was better for a while after that. Until he went to the bathroom.

He opened the door and she was standing there, on the scales. She didn't even look round when he entered. She had a towel around her, staring at her feet over the frontal bulge. He heard her groan.

'*Another two pounds, Sam. Oh God, is this how Moby Dick felt?*'

He retired early, convinced that the trauma of the day had proved more psychologically wearing than he had expected. His powers of rationalisation had been honed over the past few months of searching for a meaning to it all. So much so, that the perfume incident had now become an accepted fact, and he had resigned himself to enjoying his olfactory illusion, for that was surely what it was – there was simply no other explanation. He had stopped himself from going back into the bedroom any more for fear of smelling it again. And look at how he'd homed in on that old Alice nightmare when the lights went off.

So he was missing Jo – ah, Christ, how he still missed her – ergo he was smelling her in his bed. No visitations from across the veil. No ectoplasm on the walls. Just the old uncinate lobe playing tricks.

He fell asleep thinking that. And that night it was enough to keep Alice locked away in the dark little corner of his mind where she lurked.

But there was another thought that had insinuated

itself like a maggot in an apple. A thought that writhed and twisted and tormented his brain. Despite Paul's reassurance and dismissal, he awoke in the early hours with his mind full of doubts and imaginings about a man he'd never met. A man who'd confessed to Jo's murder.

He got up and walked into the lounge, toying with and immediately discounting another brandy. He stood at the window, looking out at a dark, silent world. Below him, behind the empty, windowless warehouse that was the sister of the one which had been already converted into the flat he now occupied, a street light flickered as the wind rattled the cable supplying it. Beyond that, the marshland swept towards the bay in a dense, black, featureless expanse. He felt immeasurably alone, more so than he had in months, and once again he called into question the wisdom of his return.

And yet, the vague feeling that had stirred in him when he'd read Debbie's letter was, if anything, stronger now. Her beseeching tone was understandable in the light of the mental turmoil she was obviously undergoing. But something else had drawn him back. Something more than simply a desire to help others affected by the tragedy of Jo's death. Debbie's words had merely augmented his own feeling of a business unfinished. Dare he say it – a premonition? He knew that Jo's death had to have some meaning. And not in the quasi-religious terms that the priest at her funeral had tried to provide. There was more to it than that and he knew, somehow, that he had a further part to play before he could lay Jo's ghost.

And that this city had the answers.

Below, as he watched, a car emerged slowly from the darkness of the marshland beyond the flickering street light. It had no lights on and moved slowly, almost silently, towards the warehouse. It was old and battered, little more than a heap. It drifted beneath him and stopped immediately below his window, its colour pale and indistinct under the sodium street lights. Sam stared

53

down at it, but saw no sign from within the dark windows. Suddenly, a strange, uncomfortable chill gripped him. A pale, featureless oval had appeared behind the darkness of the window. Whoever was inside appeared to be looking up at him. He took an involuntary step back, unnerved by the feeling of being watched, and stood there for a moment, out of sight. When he eventually crept forward again to steal a glance, there was no sign of the car.

Chapter Four

At lunchtime the following day, Sam bought flowers and drove out to the cemetery. Gaps had appeared in the thick sky, blue islands driven over by a stiff wind. Patches of low, bright sunlight seared his eyes as he drove. He donned sunglasses and felt better, not only for the protection they afforded his eyes, but for the camouflage they offered.

He didn't want anybody to see him, but for the life of him he had no real idea why. OK, admittedly it was a private thing to do, visit your dead wife for the first time since they put her in the ground with a blessing that you barely heard because of the screaming agony of guilt and denial that roared in your head. But his self-contempt at having put it off for so long was eating into him. The woman in the florist had asked him what the flowers were for and when he'd answered had fixed him with a sad sympathetic smile that had chilled him. He had almost run out of the shop.

God, what was he scared of?

The car park was full when he got there. A funeral procession was making its way from the church out into the large grounds. It was heading for the east side, some two hundred yards from where Jo lay, but still Sam didn't get out of the car. All he could do was sit there and watch. A little lying fragment of his brain said that he was doing it so as not to disturb the mourners, but his eyes told him the truth. There were at least three or four people scattered throughout the neat landscape, kneeling or standing quietly at gravestones, paying respects.

Sam looked at his hand. His palms were beaded with cold sweat. He swore at himself. Twice he picked up the flowers, but still he sat in the car and didn't get out.

He kept thinking of Alice and it annoyed him immensely to do so. She had no place in this. Her death had haunted his sleep as a child and even now his dreams never quite made it to the stage where she lay at peace in her mother's parlour, her pert, tomboy face made up to disguise the lividity and swelling that death had brought. He had seen her there. Had trembled and shaken with his mother's hand clutched firmly in his as she made him look, mindful of his troubled nights. She had wanted him to see that it was over. She had wanted him to accept the full circle of life and death.

It was the small hands arranged across the breast that had struck Sam. In life, Alice's hands had never been still.

Somewhere in the house, he had heard Alice's mother sob.

In his imagination, both conscious and unconscious, Alice laboured in eternity to escape the white tomb with three stars on the handle that they found her in. And Sam, watching the black dresses of the mourners billow in the fresh wind of that January day, could not make the connection between the past and the present. Could not understand the importance of reconciliation nor the destructiveness of guilt.

All he saw and felt was the violent trembling of his hand on the door handle every time he tried to get out. He waited until the funeral was over, but still he sat.

Finally, he reversed the car and pulled over to the verge. They were breaking into new ground near the drive that led up to the car park. Three fresh mounds of brown earth stood next to three open graves. One of them was small. A child's grave.

Quickly, he threw the flowers on the grass and drove out.   *   *   *

There was a light on in the living room of Debbie's place when he got there the following evening. It was after eleven. He'd decided to give Paul ample time to get to work and had then been afraid that he'd left it a little late to catch Debbie before she went to bed, but he needn't have worried. She opened the door dressed as if she was about to go out, or had just got in from somewhere. The blue and grey dress and the dark stockings and heels didn't look like bedtime attire.

She saw Sam's expression and laughed.

'Like I said, some days I feel fine,' she said disarmingly. 'Come in out of the cold. I've been expecting you.'

He followed her in and sat down, refused a drink and waited for Debbie to explain herself.

'I can read Paul like a book,' she said in response to his enquiring gaze. 'He's incapable of lying, did you know that? When he tries to put on a serious expression, he uses little muscles in his face that he doesn't use at any other time. I can spot it a mile off. When I asked him why he'd left for work early last night, he didn't tell me at first that he'd gone to see you. But then he admitted it. He also told me that you looked bloody awful.'

'Did he tell you why he'd called?' asked Sam.

Debbie nodded. 'And thanks for keeping our little secret.' She smiled sweetly, her eyes opening slightly, sparkling. She no longer looked the pale waif of Monday evening. She'd put on some make-up, and together with the clothes the picture of the invalid had faded somewhat. And then he remembered why he'd come.

'Who is Phipps?' he asked.

Debbie's eyes narrowed, and then she exhaled through her nose and shook her head in disbelief. 'Paul can be such an idiot sometimes.'

'He said he felt he ought to tell me.'

She walked across to the sofa next to Sam and sat down, leaning forward slightly so that she wouldn't have to speak too loudly.

'Phipps is an ex-patient of yours. He's some sort of schizophrenic. The long and the short of it is that he gave himself up two months after you'd gone away.' She paused. 'As Jo's murderer.'

'That's what Paul said.'

'Of course, there was nothing in it. He'd read about the case and many of the details. I think he'd convinced himself that he'd done it, but there was no hard evidence. The man had been institutionalised two or three times. It was only after five or six days of enquiry that his medical history came to light. As Paul would say, the chap was so far round the bend, he was meeting himself on the way back.'

'But why?'

'Oh Sam, don't do this to yourself now. There was absolutely nothing in it, really.'

'But why didn't you tell me?' he demanded.

'Tell you what? Paul says that at least three lunatics confess to every murder. What good would telling you have done?'

Sam shook his head in confusion. The world was suddenly upside down again.

'Sam, listen to me. I know what this is doing to you. I went through exactly the same thing. Shock – bewilderment – anger. But I've seen this man and believe me, he's a crank.'

'You've seen him?'

She sighed. 'Yes. I made Paul take me down to the station. It was not a very pleasant experience.'

'Didn't he give any explanation as to why he confessed?'

Debbie paused, avoiding Sam's gaze. 'He said that the mother of Jesus had told him to kill the devil that was in Jo.'

The awfulness, the terrible, unfair insanity of it struck Sam like a fist. It was his baby they were talking about. His and Jo's. A pure, unsullied life, cocooned and safe inside his mother's womb, snuffed out by some maniac.

Sam knew where the evil lay, it was in the black soul of whoever had done that to Jo and . . .

'Sam?'

Through the muzzy mental cloud that had descended over him, Sam heard Debbie's voice. It sounded far away, so far away.

'Sam? Are you all right?'

'Yes,' he said and realised he was crying. 'Yes, I'm fine.' There was no noise, just silent salty tears that sprung from his eyes and trickled into his mouth. He felt weak and helpless again. In the face of such atrocious words, his resistance had crumbled like age-old mortar.

'Sam, Jo knows how much you cared,' said Debbie earnestly.

He looked up and nodded. 'I could smell her yesterday. When I got home from work, she was in the bedroom. Her smell was on the pillow.'

He saw Debbie staring at him, he saw her eyes fill with the gleam that he'd seen and been wary of before. He checked himself mentally, the realisation of what he'd said suddenly dawning. 'God, listen to me. I sound like bloody Phipps.'

'Don't say that,' said Debbie angrily. 'Don't ever say that.' And then her voice changed, softened. 'Don't you see? It was Jo. I knew it would happen, I knew it.'

Sam held up his hand in protest. Even in his current state of turmoil, there was only so much he could accept. 'Hold on a minute. There are such things as olfactory hallucinations. Being back in this city, seeing the same places that Jo and I used to go to, seeing the people we used to meet, seeing you. It's bound to trigger off memories and sometimes . . . sometimes the mind can play some very fancy tricks.'

'Is that what you really believe?'

Sam shrugged.

Debbie leaned further forward and looked into Sam's eyes. He could smell her. She wore a different perfume from Jo, less musky. She took one of Sam's hands in hers and held it in her lap. 'You have to accept this,' she said quietly. 'I struggled against it too, at first. But it is Jo, I know it is. She's trying to tell us something, Sam. And I know she's going to succeed. But we have to believe in her, Sam. We have to believe.'

Sam turned his face away, unable to hold the fierce conviction of her gaze. Debbie's hand, cool and smooth like Jo's, brought his face back round to meet her eyes, and when she spoke, her words were strange and enigmatic. 'You have to do what you feel is right, Sam.'

He was never quite sure how it happened, but later he wondered if subconsciously he hadn't really wanted it. His hands came up to Debbie's breasts, firm yet soft through the material of her dress. Her fingers entwined his hair and their mouths met full of yearning and wanting. He lost himself in the embrace for what seemed like hours, his mind, somehow freed of reason, convinced him that he was holding Jo again. It was Jo's breasts he was cupping, Jo's tongue that was dancing in his mouth, her thigh his hand was stroking, her flesh his fingers seeked.

And then, like an arrow striking its target, his mind thudded back into sanity and reason. He pulled back and lurched up, almost beside himself with anguish, his hands, palms forward, held up in a gesture of apology, his eyes wide with the horror of what had happened.

'Debbie,' he croaked entreatingly. 'My God, Debbie. I'm sorry . . . I'm sorry.'

Debbie sat where she was with colour flaming her cheeks, her breathing rapid, lips still parted from the kiss, and smiled. In the smile was forgiveness and understanding and something else that Sam could not quite fathom. 'Don't apologise, Sam, not to me. You don't have to. I understand.'

'I, uh . . . I could do with a drink,' said Sam, running a finger around the inside of his shirt collar.

Debbie supplied him with a whisky and he took a couple of healthy swallows, which helped. He drained the glass and Debbie refilled it without speaking. She didn't have anything herself – probably because of the ME, he thought. Alcohol was meant to make things worse. He remembered Paul's anxiety of the day before and realised guiltily that he still hadn't phoned Debbie's GP, or asked Debbie any of the questions he had meant to ask her. But he couldn't bring himself to talk about her desire, or rather her recent lack of desire, to have children now. It was neither the time nor the place. Paul would simply have to wait.

He left shortly afterwards, a hurried, embarrassed exit. He felt foolish driving back to the flat. Foolish and confused. What the hell did he think he was doing? He would have to be careful, he knew that. To take his mind off the incident with Debbie, he thought of Phipps. He couldn't remember anything about him, yet Debbie had said he was an old patient of his. He desperately tried to remember if there had been some sort of friction between them. Was that why he'd confessed and said those things? Could it have been Phipps who had superglued the car locks? It seemed petty compared with confessing to a murder, but then neither seemed to be the work of a balanced mind. The thought was not a comfortable one.

By the time Sam got back to the flat, he knew that he'd have to lay the ghost that Phipps had suddenly become if he was to have any peace of mind about the affair.

Sam spent the weekend on menial chores, none of which were vital, but which were nonetheless necessary for him to function properly. He ordered newpapers, reopened a charge account at his local garage, got up early to catch the milkman and generally tried to reintegrate himself. On Wednesday, he spent an hour in the library searching through September's *Echo*. He found the story in the September 28th edition. It had made the front page. But it wasn't until five days later that they had actually named him. By that time the story's slant had changed from a character assassination of Phipps to a damning indictment of the police's ineptitude. But it gave Sam more than enough information. Reading again the lurid details of Jo's death simply fanned the fire of his troubled mind.

It was Thursday lunchtime before Sam had an opportunity to talk to Lambourne. Greychapel psychiatric hospital was on the other side of town. He sat at the back of a poorly ventilated room listening to Lambourne chair a session of case presentations for half an hour, and remained there while the staff gradually filed out until only he and Lambourne were left. They'd never met, but Sam had communicated by letter several times. Sam studied him. He was a short man with a grey-flecked beard and a pale face dominated by an arrogant, almost hooked nose. It was a strong face, full of assurance and character, as befitted his consultant status. He looked up from the papers he was gathering on the desk.

'Ah,' he said, holding up one finger. 'Dr Croxley, isn't it?'

'Crawford,' said Sam as he walked over and shook Lambourne's hand. 'You got my message then?'

'I did. Have a seat.' He pointed to one of the grey plastic chairs and Sam sat down again.

'My secretary said you wanted to talk to me about Dorian Phipps.'

Sam nodded. 'Two days ago I learned that Phipps confessed to my wife's murder. I want to know why he did it.'

Lambourne watched Sam, his face suddenly wary. 'I don't know whether we should discuss this. I'm not quite sure it's ethical.'

'Look,' said Sam. 'Phipps is a patient of mine. I've been through my files and find that I saw him for a sore throat eight months before Jo was killed. That's all. I'd not seen him before, and haven't seen him since. Then I find out he's confessed to Jo's murder. Bugger the ethics. I want to know why he did that.'

Lambourne sighed and played with the papers on his desk consideringly. 'All right,' he said finally. He took a file half an inch thick from a pile on the seat beside him and opened it. 'Dorian Phipps, aged thirty-eight. He presented eight years ago. He was unmarried and holding down a job at that time. Both parents are dead, but he has a sister somewhere. His initial psychotic episode was mild. Here, read the letter he wrote to his sister before he was admitted the first time.'

Sam took the notes and studied a typewritten page.

Dear Angela,
    I know who is interfering with the television. The women at work are involved. I saw them passing round a magazine yesterday. It had my photograph in it, I'm sure. I heard one of them say 'He looks different on the TV.' I know now that they must be watching me at night from the TV set. They interfere with my bowels. Perhaps I could have an operation to give me back the control of my bladder, but I doubt that the TV would allow it. If you have any influence with the Roman Catholites, perhaps you could speak to them. I find the intrusion intolerable.

        Yours sincerely,
        Dorian

Sam looked up at Lambourne. The letter was disturbing, but all Lambourne did was shrug and say, 'Fairly typical.'

'Is it?'

'Oh, I'm sorry, I assumed . . . Yes it is, take it from me. He has a classic paranoid subtype schizophrenia. The letter shows typical delusional obsessions with religion and radiation exerting some influence over his life. He'd established a niche for himself in society, but had always been considered reserved and tense by his colleagues – even at school. He left work after sending the letter to his sister and his behaviour became increasingly bizarre. We hospitalised him for about six months and established reasonable control with phenothiazines. He's had two acute paranoic episodes since that time, necessitating admission on both occasions. Overall, he's been pretty stable.'

'Then how do you explain his actions?'

Lambourne stood up, walked to the board at the head of the room and wrote PHARMACOTHERAPY in red. 'There, I think, is your answer. Schizophrenics are often the near misses of society. It's no accident that geniuses often show schizophrenic-type traits. Schizophrenics have an increased responsiveness to sensory and emotional stimulation. Their sensitivity is so great that they can't suppress the input enough to minimise its effect. If they could, they might turn out to be brilliantly creative, but unfortunately most of them can't and their response is therefore to withdraw. Drugs,' he pointed to the word he'd written on the board again, 'work by helping to dampen down the excessive input. They literally "dull" the senses.'

Sam nodded. 'And if he stopped taking the drugs, the delusions would recur.'

'Exactly,' said Lambourne. 'Phipps was very paranoid when he was readmitted after his "confession". He claimed that some religious force had made him stop the medication. He is still not fully controlled.'

'Someone glued all the locks in my car a few days ago. Could that have been Phipps?'

Lambourne's face clouded. 'No, I don't think so. He's not exactly locked in here, but usually all he does is ride his bicycle around the grounds. He feels very threatened outside the confines of the hospital.' Lambourne studied Sam's sceptical face and added, 'You must understand that his actions were not aimed at you specifically. He deluded himself into believing that he committed this crime. The real crime was all the media coverage that instilled the thought into his head. I doubt he even knows who you are.'

'I'd like to see him,' said Sam.

Lambourne considered the request at length and finally said, 'No, I'm sorry. I don't think that would be a good idea.'

'Why not for God's sake?'

'Because your reaction is likely to be emotional and the effect on Phipps might be adverse.'

'For crying out loud, I only want to speak to him. To convince myself of what everyone else is saying.'

'No. I don't think so.'

'You don't think so! Don't you understand what all this is doing to me? I have to know, can't you see that? I have to be sure.' Sam could hear his voice rising.

Lambourne remained unmoved. 'I appreciate all of that, and I'm sorry. But I have to think of Dorian Phipps. He is still an in-patient here and as long as he is, I think that any visit from you will be detrimental. I'm sorry.'

Lambourne stood up and closed Phipp's file. Gathering up his papers, he bade Sam a tight-lipped farewell.

There was a message waiting for Sam when he got back to the surgery. It was from a Mr Urquart's secretary. It had sounded important and they wanted him to ring back. Sam didn't know anyone called Urquart, but he rang anyway.

'Good afternoon,' sang the secretary when he got through. 'Urquart Insurance. Can I help you?'

'Insurance?' groaned Sam. 'Thanks, but no thanks.' He heard Urquart's secretary catch her breath and demanded, 'Who *is* this?'

The voice changed, became quieter and hesitant. 'It's Chloe . . . I promise not to try and sell you anything.'

Sam felt a smile steal over his lips. 'Sorry,' he said and added, 'tough morning. And how is Mr Urquart today?'

'Out to lunch,' said Chloe. 'I thought I'd phone to thank you for the flowers and for returning the car.'

'It's me that should be thanking you. I'm sorry. I really

65

have been meaning to phone. It's been one of those weeks, I'm afraid.'

'Oh, please. I know how busy you are. Jo used to . . .' The sentence petered out. 'I'm sorry. I have this knack of managing to say the wrong thing.'

'Don't apologise. It might do you some good to talk about her if it's that much of a hang-up for you.'

'Oh, no, I . . .'

'Look, perhaps it would do us both good. Why don't we meet up?' He heard the silence on the line and imagined the consternation on her face.

'Uhh, I suppose it would be all right.'

'Only if you want to,' said Sam quickly.

'I do. But only if you're my guest.'

'There's no need –'

'I insist,' she said and there was something in her voice that made Sam not object further. Perhaps it gave her the handle she needed to control the situation.

'OK, fine.'

He had felt bad about not contacting Chloe; it was unforgivable after she'd saved the day by lending him her car. He was the one who should be asking her out to dinner. His thoughts turned automatically to Jo, but he surprised himself by consciously not letting his guilt get the upper hand. He suddenly realised that despite all his reservations, he liked Chloe. And it was as good a way as any to stop himself from thinking too much about Debbie and Phipps.

'Uhh, when?' he asked finally.

'Tonight? I could pick you up at seven-thirty. If you'll give me an address,' she said, sounding pleased.

Sam gave it to her and as he put the phone down, he experienced something it took him a while to understand simply because it had been so rare in his life for so long. A faint fluttering in his chest of something that had lain like a chrysallis for months – a feeling of pleasurable anticipation.

Chapter Five

Dinner with Chloe was full of surprises.

'Do you like fish and chips?' she asked, staring up at him from inside her car and making it sound as if the ratification of a UN directive depended upon his response.

'Fine,' said Sam as he climbed in, not quite sure if he really did see a mischievous bunching of the muscles under her eyes.

'Good,' she said enigmatically and drove them out to a restaurant called Flaherty's somewhere on the A48. There was a sign announcing 'Fish and Chips' in blue neon over the door, but any similarity between Flaherty's and a high-street chippy evaporated there. Inside were marble-topped tables and wooden church forms. Waiters wrapped in fishmongers' aprons dashed about as if it was a busy day at Billingsgate. On the way in, Sam stepped over a small bridge, underneath which was an ornamental pool full of twitching lobsters. The place was heaving, but a hostess led Sam and Chloe to an upstairs table, and Sam, who was delighted with the surroundings, found himself equally beguiled by the langoustines and salmon steak that followed.

Chloe was obviously gratified by Sam's approval of the restaurant, but he couldn't help noticing her unease in the crowded space. She drank mineral water as an aperitif and as she fidgeted with her napkin and looked around at every diner in the place to the exclusion of Sam himself, he again wondered what it was that had so sapped her confidence.

Watching her people-watching was not an arduous task and the more he did so, the more enigmatic she seemed. There was no physical reason for her diffidence, certainly not from where he was sitting. The shapeless camouflage she preferred for daily sorties into the urban jungle had been replaced by elegance and grace. And here, Sam felt, was the real animal. Hers was not the gaudy flamboyance of the impulsive fashion buyer, nor the well-worn dowdiness of the curmudgeon. This was tasteful and simple, yet somehow exotic. If she didn't actually stop conversations as she walked by, she certainly slowed them down. She drew stares like a magnet, but strangely enough, although it was often men who turned their heads, it was women who ogled. As he'd followed her in, he'd heard one lady whisper enviously to her partner as she pointed to Chloe's dress, 'That's a Famigliani. I pointed it out to you in Bath last week, but I don't suppose you took any notice.'

Sam deliberately did most of the talking and, gratifyingly, Chloe slowly began to emerge from her shell. They talked mostly of Jo. The conversation was not strained or forced, time enough had passed for Sam and it was obvious that Chloe had bottled up a tide of feeling.

'Jo liked it here,' she said suddenly.

'I didn't know she'd been.'

'We had lunch here a couple of times.'

Sam nodded. 'She enjoyed your lunches together.'

'Did you mind?'

'Mind? No. Jo was a free spirit.'

'She really loved you for giving her that.'

'Did she?'

Chloe nodded. 'It's a rare thing in a relationhip. Something to treasure.'

Sam half frowned and was thinking of what next to say when the waiter arrived. With the meal came a bottle of white burgundy and gradually Chloe began to unwind. Just before dessert, he complimented her on the dress.

68

'Thank you. I'm glad you like it,' she said, accepting gracefully, and Sam noted gratifyingly, that for once she didn't let her eyes linger on his face, searching for the sarcasm she obviously expected.

Somebody did this to you, didn't they? thought Sam. *Somebody I don't think I would particularly like very much.*

'Who is Famigliani anyway?' he asked innocently.

'How did you know?' she gasped.

'Oh, I read all the best magazines.'

'Oh yes?' she said sceptically.

'Actually, I heard someone commenting on it earlier – a mixture of admiration and covetousness. It must be expensive.'

'Reasonably,' she said, colour flaring at her throat. 'And I suppose you're wondering how a temporary secretary can afford such a thing?'

'It hadn't crossed my mind for an instant,' said Sam, grinning at the challenge in her eyes.

After a moment, she dropped her gaze. 'I have a weakness for good clothes. I've learned on my travels that some things are worth paying for. I bought it in Italy.'

Sam raised his eyebrows speculatively. 'You've travelled a lot, then?'

She hesitated the merest fraction before saying, 'I haven't always been a secretary or a redundant travel agent. I used to be an air hostess.'

'Jo never told me that.'

'I . . . I asked her not to.'

'Why?' laughed Sam.

Chloe shook her head dismissively. 'It's too stereo-typing.'

'Is it?'

'Oh come on.' She had hunched forward again, her hair swinging forward in a curve that framed her threatened eyes.

'I have no preconceptions. In fact, you're the first one I've met outside of a cabin. Why did you leave? Jet lag catch up with you?' he speculated.

She smiled thinly. 'You could say that. I used to be on long-haul – 747s from London to everywhere. I had some personal problems with another member of the airline and . . .' She shook her head and shrugged.

'I'm sorry,' said Sam genuinely.

'And now I'm a secretary,' she said with mock cheeriness. 'Back in a city which holds happy teenage memories. I daresay my return had something to do with trying to find that happiness again.'

'It must be very different.'

'Different, and safe.'

Sam nodded, wondering only slightly at her choice of words. 'Parents?' he asked.

'Divorced and both caught up in second marriages. When I told my mother I'd left the airline she said I must be mad.' The laugh died on her face as she realised self-consciously what she was saying.

'Perhaps we all are,' said Sam quietly.

They ate sorbet as dessert and Chloe paid. Sam sensed that a macho insistence on footing the bill would cut no ice with Miss Jesson, so he thanked her graciously for the meal and invited her back to the flat for coffee.

Her hesitation was momentary but definite.

'If you'd rather not, I can get a taxi.'

'No, that's ridiculous. I'd like to.'

In the car, Sam asked about Ned Whelan.

'Why ask about him?' she frowned.

'The other morning, when you came to see me at the surgery, I caught him staring at you in the waiting room.'

She made a face. 'I tried to ignore him. I was hoping no one would notice.'

'Why?'

'Why did I ignore him, or why was he staring?'

'Both.'

She stretched both arms out on the driving wheel, arched her back and sighed. 'I ignored him because that's how I treat all things I despise. He was staring at me because I was sitting in your queue, I expect.'

'Sorry?'

'Look, I don't want to compromise one of your colleagues.'

'None of this will go any further.'

'You say that now, but . . .' She paused, agonising over whether to go on, but finally she seemed to make up her mind. 'When I came to see you the day Jo died –'

Sam nodded. 'You came for your smear result.'

'It was Jo that suggested I come.'

'What do you mean?'

'Remember where you found it?'

Sam pondered for a moment. 'In Ned's desk.'

'Hidden', she said, pausing for effect, 'at the bottom.'

'Well lost, anyway.'

Chloe's left eybrow arched sceptically. 'I don't like Dr Whelan. I expect you've gathered that. He was nice enough at first, nice and very helpful. I had a cold. It was shortly after I'd left the airline and I was pretty run-down. He took some blood, listened to my chest – oh, he was very thorough. Then I had an eye infection and again he was most sympathetic, insisted on listening to my chest again, in case there was "residual infection", and took a swab from my eye. Then I had the smear. Dr Manton took it in the well women's clinic. I knew Dr Whelan knew I was there that day. He'd waved to me as I sat in the waiting room. I pretended not to see him, but . . .' She shook her head.

'Something happened while Dr Manton took the smear. I suddenly heard Dr Whelan's voice from the doorway. From where I was lying I couldn't see, but I do remember that Dr Manton became very angry at Dr Whelan for coming in unannounced like that, especially as we were in the middle of the smear. I didn't think too much of it at the time, but later . . . Dr Manton said the test would be back in a couple of weeks, so I made an appointment to see Dr Whelan. I duly turned up, only to find that the result wasn't back. But he sat me down and we had a long chat and it didn't seem too bad. I went back a week later, and still it wasn't back. This happened on a further two occasions, by which time I was getting worried. I began wondering if they were keeping my test at the laboratory because there was something dreadfully wrong with it.'

Sam nodded. Chloe was the last person to whom that sort of delay should have happened. With her anxiety level, it was like throwing rocket fuel on to a bonfire.

'And then, the last time I went to see Dr Whelan, he apologised and we chatted and he began to ask me about my leisure time, and what I did to relax. It took me a while to twig that he was trying to proposition me. It came as such a shock that I felt sick. I was really worried about the smear by then, and here was this lizard thing asking me if I wanted to go out for a drink. I remembered him coming in while I was having the smear and all of a sudden it all felt very wrong. Wrong and somehow dirty and horrible. That was when Jo had the idea of me seeing you. I lied about when I'd seen him last. It was actually the day before I saw you.'

Sam exhaled audibly.

'I don't want to make a fuss and I know what it sounds like. But I also don't ever want to see *him* again. I think he held that test back deliberately.'

'It could have been a genuine mistake. He could have put that result in the drawer by accident.'

'Was his reaction in the waiting room an accident?'

Sam shook his head, remembering what Peta Manton had said about Ned's recent domestic upheaval, as well as his strange reaction to Sam's return.

'And I'll tell you something else,' went on Chloe, her cheeks flaming, 'I wasn't the only one he kept bringing back for results.'

'What does that mean?' asked Sam.

'You tell me. Look, I really don't want to get anyone into trouble. In fact, I feel a little sorry for him. But I think he's taking advantage of his position. Taking liberties. I think he's going to have to be very careful.'

Sam stared at her, but her face remained inscrutable. 'What exactly do you – '

'No,' said Chloe, I'm not going to say any more. I'll let you make up your own mind,' and from the set of her jaw, Sam could see that she had closed the book on the subject. What she'd said was disquieting enough, and it had crystallised some feelings he himself had had about Ned. Her words made him feel very uncomfortable.

Chloe came up to the flat for coffee. They talked, but mostly she wandered around, picking up objet's d'art and admiring furniture that Jo and she had either chosen or talked about. Pretty soon, Ned Whelan was forgotten. When Chloe began to make leaving noises just after the chimes of midnight had rung from a clock somewhere in the city, Sam found himself reluctant to see her go. He realised with a jolt that he was very attracted to her. He had enjoyed her company immensely and he found himself telling her as much.

'We'll have to do this again, this time on me,' he said. She replied with a nod and a tight little smile that he interpreted as her version of enthusiasm.

'I'll ring you,' he said.

'I'm in most nights,' she said and he found her words strangely reassuring. 'If not, you can always ring me at work.'

'Won't Mr Urquart mind?' he teased.

Chloe smiled. 'I doubt it. Answering the phone is not his favourite occupation.'

He took her down to her car and kissed her chastely on the cheek as he held open the door for her.

Watching her go, his body cooling as the wind whistled through his shirt, Sam allowed himself a rueful smile. He had glimpsed another side of Jo that evening. A side he knew little about. A side that had its own loyalty, female companionship, private confidences. He wasn't angry, but he had the impression that Chloe had half expected him to be. She seemed ultra-sensitive to every nuance. Even so, he'd been more relaxed than in months.

Upstairs, he started clearing away the coffee cups and as he knelt to pick up a spoon he'd dropped, he noticed a pile of magazines behind a chair. Puzzled, he walked over and picked up the top copy. He stared at it in bewilderment. It was a *Vogue*, dated May '91'. There was something familiar about the dazzling smile that beamed out from the cover. Had it caught his eye in the surgery amongst the torn copies of *House and Garden* and *Options* that littered the waiting room?

Like the sudden clearing of fog on a road, his mind broke through and he knew where he'd seen that self-same pile of magazines only days before during his unpacking. They'd rested, half hidden behind a pile of shoes, at the bottom of a wardrobe. Jo's wardrobe. Magazines had been Jo's one vice. *Cosmo, Vogue, Ideal Home*. She was eclectic in the extreme. As long as it was glossy.

Falteringly, he took the pile over to the sofa, spreading them thickly next to him. He opened the *Vogue*, his hands trembling. It looked almost new, free of dust. He felt sweat, cold like winter rain, trickle down his neck and soak into his shirt. The magazine fell open towards the centre, where the corners of several pages had been neatly turned down to mark the place. Sam stared at the photograph on the page: a woman, naked from the waist up, embracing a similarly unattired infant. 'Baby-bonding – Medical fact or Fiction' announced the heading. It was standard stuff, quoting the most recent pronouncements of a variety of eminent psychologists. Sam knew that it would probably be rehashed in a few months time when the topic re-emerged as a medical talking-point.

He put down the *Vogue* and picked up a copy of *Options*. He noticed the date: April, a month before the *Vogue*. He thumbed through it and found another page with a turned-down corner. This time it marked a full page advertisement for a moisturiser. The implication was that use of the energising cream would rejuvenate

74

the skin, making it as clear and soft as a baby's. It was banal copy, but the visual comparison between the model's flawless skin and that of the baby she was holding was stunning.

It wasn't until the fourth magazine, and another advert starring a giggling baby ostensibly approving of its mother's use of a fabric softener, that the penny finally dropped for Sam. Struggling to find the link between the articles and adverts in the magazines, he had concentrated on the product. Suddenly, with a mental lurch, his growing subconscious apprehension was precipitated into a realisation.

Babies. Mothers and babies.

His child?

His mouth suddenly filled with saline and sweat oozed out of his brow. He dashed for the bathroom, where he gagged and finally succumbed to the nausea, depositing the supper he had enjoyed so much with Chloe in a spattering heap in the toilet bowl. Afterwards, he sat slumped on the floor, his hands cradling the bowl, his body weak with the exertion of vomiting, his mind struggling to find some sort of tenable explanation for it all. First the perfume, now magazines full of pictures of mothers and children. What was going on?

Had he imagined seeing them before?

He stood and stumbled to the bedroom, tearing open the wardrobe door. Hanging up were Jo's clothes, and lining the floor, neatly arranged, were her shoes. Behind them, in a corner towards the back of what was in truth a walk-in wardrobe, was a neat space the exact size of a magazine.

He'd seen them there. That was where Jo had kept them until the pile grew large enough to merit a biannual clear out. So how had they moved?

Had he gone through them and marked each page that suggested things that might have been? Had he taken part in some sub-conscious orgy of memory and yearning, or even moved them in his sleep? He knew with absolute certainty that until he'd seen them that evening, he had not consciously registered their presence in the room. So what did that make him? Just a little bit crazy, or stark raving mad? What else could he have been doing without knowing anything about it? The feeling left him dazed. But there seemed little in the way of feasible alternatives. If he hadn't put them there, who else, or what else, could possibly –

His thoughts abruptly swung to Debbie. He knew instinctively what she would have said, and for an instant he contemplated it. Could it have been Jo? Jo trying to talk to him? Even thinking of it sent a shudder through him. She was dead. *Dead* for God's sake, and so was his unborn child. It was Debbie who was the crazy one. Debbie and this bloody town who were sending him up the wall. So his mind was playing tricks on him? OK. Fine. That was all right. As long as he had insight, it was OK . . . Wasn't it?

Well, it had to stop, he knew that.

He stood up and splashed cold water on his face and then brushed the vomit from his teeth. He went back into the lounge, picked up the magazines and took them into the second bedroom, where he dumped them unceremoniously into a cardboard box.

He went back into the lounge, poured himself a small brandy and drank it in one. It tasted odd after the toothpaste and felt leaden in his tender stomach, but he kept it down and followed it with another. He thought of Chloe and of the strength and resolve she'd shown in the face of her own personal adversity. It gave him hope. Perhaps one day he would tell her all about this. It would be good to talk to someone else. He wondered whether madness was contagious. Perhaps he'd been spending too much time with Debbie. And then he chided himself. That was ridiculous. Debbie couldn't help it. He ought to be doing something to help her. He still hadn't rung her GP. He felt sure she would get over this nonsense about Jo once her ME was better. What chance did she have mentally if her defences were being sapped by a physical illness? One had to get rid of diseased tissue if the body was to heal.

And then, inexorably, and for the thousandth time that day, he thought of Phipps. Phipps was like a disease, too. A disease inside Sam, gnawing away at his mind, proliferating like some virulent agent, creating a tumour of doubt. Was Phipps what all this was about? Could the spectre of Phipps be poisoning his mind enough to cause him to do something as inexplicable as the magazines? Gradually, uncontrollably, he felt his anger building, layer upon layer of rage and frustration, pent up over months.

She was dead.

D.E.A.D.

Couldn't everyone accept that? Couldn't he?

The *Vogue* he'd picked up initially still lay on the seat where he'd discarded it. He lunged at it and began tearing at it, ripping it to shreds, saliva flying from his mouth with the effort. He held it lengthwise, the spine down, twisting and wrenching to rupture it. It gave easily and he rent it, grasping pages by the handful, raving and violent, until the thing was a mere pile of shredded paper.

A moan of anguish leaped from his throat and he crashed his hand down on to the glass-topped coffee table, shattering it into three large, jagged pieces.

The noise exploding in his ears and the jarring pain in his hand shook him back to sanity.

He sat heavily, staring down at the destruction he had wreaked, his arms weak and trembling from adrenaline. He sat there for a long while, pondering the inescapable thoughts that played on his mind like a maddening tune.

He remembered what Lambourne had said, and yet it wasn't enough.

In his hands there were pieces of the ripped magazine and a ballpoint that had been on the coffee table. As his mind had wandered, he had doodled. Most of the scribbles contained just one word.

A name.

Phipps.

He knew then that he had to see for himself. Had to be sure that it could not have been Phipps who had done those things to Jo. The idea grew in him like a jungle vine until it choked all other thoughts from his mind. He had to see him. Had to set his turbulent mind at rest. And suddenly, the decision made, he felt better.

Sod Lambourne, he would see Phipps.

He would go and see Phipps for himself.

Chapter Six

Sam awoke with a headache. It came as no surprise. His night's sleep had been fitful and troubled. Twice he'd woken from some disturbing dream, the memory of which had mercifully fled the minute he'd become conscious. But the feeling of unease it left him with was uncomfortable enough. He'd lain awake in the black, silent hours listening to the eerie bleat of a foghorn calling out its warning to those who cared to listen. It sounded like a wretched animal mourning a dead mate and in the darkness he mourned with it, shackled by his guilt to the painful memory of those he had loved and lost:

Alice, his cousin, the hapless victim of her own irrepressible inquisitiveness.

His father and mother, victims of diseases that he, a doctor, had been powerless to arrest.

And Jo, whose death haunted him the worst of all in those unholy hours when his mind could not escape into everyday distractions. When it could not be deceived into believing that there was reason and hope. In those hours, there was nothing but the gaping abyss of emptiness where once there had been Jo.

There was nothing new in these nocturnal thoughts, they had plagued him along with insomnia at the beginning, when his grief had been most acute. But gradually, with time, untroubled sleep had returned and with it had come release for his tortured mind. These days, it needed some particularly painful reminder or upset to bring the nightmares back. And in the darkness,

Sam didn't have to ponder long over the reason for their return that night.

Phipps.

His faceless image hovered wraith-like over Sam's poorly remembered dreams, intangible and haunting, drip-feeding doubt into his brain. And during that long, endless night, his desire to exorcise the ghost that Phipps had become to him hardened into an iron resolve.

At work, Peta Manton stopped by his room and said he looked pale. Even the ever-dapper Jack Rioch – whose pace of life left little time for social niceties, and who had consequently been nicknamed JR (as in Jack Russell) by Peta – commented on how tired he looked. His response to both was to arch his back, bare his teeth in an arid smile and implicate a new and particularly hard bed as the culprit.

The morning clinic was busy and his lunchtime was spent collecting his own car from the garage that had been servicing it and returning the hired transport.

By late afternoon, things had quietened down enough for him to be able to walk into the waiting room without being pinned to the wall by visual lances in his back from queueing patients. He strolled over to the reception desk and glanced around. Jack Rioch had disappeared off on a golfing weekend and Peta had gone to a conference on a child abuse case. Sam's last two patients were just arriving and there were three waiting outside Ned Whelan's door. Sam studied them casually. Two were elderly and so muffled against the weather as to be unrecognisable as anything other than two untidy bundles of clothes that occasionally moved, and the third was a young woman in jeans and a chunky sweater, restlessly thumbing magazines.

Sam went back to his room and sorted out his final two of the afternoon: a three-month-old baby whose mother was sure she had a squint and a young man with three days' stubble and a croaky, bubbly cold who needed nothing more than plenty of fluids, reassurance and a warm bed.

When he stepped back out into the waiting area, Sam noticed that both bundles of woollies and the chunky sweater had gone from outside Ned's door. As he stood there, he saw another woman of about thirty enter and walk up to the reception desk. She was well dressed, almost overdressed for a mere visit to the surgery. Sam surmised that she must have come directly from work. He watched as she exchanged pleasantries with the ever-polite Brenda and saw her turn in the direction of Ned Whelan's door. It was late, five-thirty by his watch. Surgery officially ended at five-thirty. He walked over to Brenda, who greeted him with her customary smile.

'Ned working late?' he asked innocently.

'Oh yes, he's very good like that now. Fits people in if it's inconvenient for them to come during working hours. He's often here after I've gone home,' she said, making it sound the most natural thing in the world.

'Not like the old Ned I knew,' said Sam. 'Used to be able to set my watch by Ned's five-thirty twenty-yard dash to the door.'

'Just goes to show how people mellow with age, Dr Crawford,' said Brenda, her eyes twinkling with scepticism.

'Don't I know that girl who just came in?' asked Sam.

'Lucy Kendrick? I don't think so . . .'

Sam turned the appointments book around and looked at Lucy Kendrick's name and the name written below it of the patient yet to come – also female. Brenda took out Lucy's file and handed it to Sam. He took it and read the last entry. It had SMEAR stamped in red ink and next to it a tick.

'No,' said Sam, shaking his head and handing the notes back to Brenda. 'Not the girl I was thinking of.'

The phone rang and Brenda turned to answer it. She had already placed the file of the woman due after Lucy Kendrick on the desk in readiness. Sam picked it up and read the last entry. The red stamp was identical to Lucy Kendrick's. He replaced the notes on the desk before Brenda had even noticed and returned to his room. Glancing back, he saw Ned Whelan emerge from his own room, stride over to the desk and pick up two sets of case notes. Smiling, he ushered Lucy Kendrick into his room. There was a hint of welcome on his lips, but it twisted into a wintery grimace as his eyes briefly met Sam's.

Back at his desk, Sam wrote down the names of both women in his diary. He almost stopped himself halfway through doing it, embarrassed by the cloak-and-dagger nature of it all. But something, an inner urge, made him carry on. It instinctively seemed the right thing to do.

He turned to his terminal and typed in Phipps's name. It took ten seconds for the details to scroll up. The correspondence was extensive, transferred from the easily lost and cumbersome paper it had been written on by the hand scanners that Brenda and her staff now used automatically when storing information in the computer as well as in the huge filing room at the rear of the building. It looked as if it was Ned who had mainly dealt with the minor ailments that had driven Phipps to attend – an ear infection, bronchitis, a back injury caused by a fall from his bicycle. But underneath all of this was the documentation – extensive and detailed – of Lambourne's continuing battle to keep Phipps sane.

Sam chose the three most recent letters and instructed the small desktop bubblejet printer to give him some hard copies. It was as the machine was pushing out the second letter that someone knocked and immediately entered.

'Peta. . . ?' stammered Sam.

She stood on the threshold, a mildly accusatory expression on her flushed cheeks. She wore a coat that had glistening drops of rain on the shoulders.

'Forgot my bleep. And guess what I heard as I passed your door?'

'Just finishing off a few things.'

'Sam, you look bushed.'

'I'm fine,' said Sam. She couldn't see his VDU from where she stood. She would undoubtedly have known about Phipps and Sam didn't want any more good advice about his preoccupation.

Peta looked across at the printer and then back at Sam.

'OK. No lectures. I'm not going to waste my breath asking you if you want to come over tonight for dinner with Dick and me . . .' She let it hang in the air.

'Uhhhh . . .'

'I know. I know. Too soon. You need time to settle in. And maybe you're right. It takes a lot of stamina to sit and listen to Dick's politics all night. But promise me you'll take things easy this weekend, Sam?'

'Feet up, honestly.'

Peta stood there with her eyebrows arched sceptically.

Sam got up and gathered together the sheets of copied letters. He stuffed them into his briefcase and switched off the computer dramatically.

'There,' he said.

Peta walked out of the building with him, convinced she had done her good deed for the day.

Greychapel's squat buildings and stark tree-lined grounds looked almost deserted as Sam made his way across the car park. It wasn't by mere luck that it appeared thus. He'd deliberately chosen a Saturday afternoon in order to minimise the likelihood of encountering medical staff. And since the January sales were in full swing, the number of visitors was likely to be small too.

He made for an entrance above which a blue and white sign announced: ALL VISITORS MUST REPORT HERE.

It was a freezing, windless day. The weak January sun had failed miserably in its attempt to penetrate the quilt of gun-metal cloud that blanketed the sky and hung

83

greyly over the misted horizon. Across to his right, Sam watched a solitary figure shamble along a gravelled path. The man, of indeterminable age but who appeared ancient largely due to his stooping, shuffling gait, was making agonisingly slow progress. He reminded Sam of an extra from *Night of the Zombies*, or one of its like. The sort of film where the living dead manage to capture innumerable lithe and nimble young girls despite being able to travel no faster than two miles an hour on wooden legs.

It was a needlessly melodramatic analogy, but it sprang to mind unbidden and Sam was on the point of laughing at himself when the shambling man stopped and, turning towards a blasted elm tree, began shouting and blathering, his previously loose and dangling arms suddenly animated and flailing. Sam couldn't make out the content of the man's tirade, but he watched his words streaming out in spiralling clouds of water vapour as his breath condensed in the cold air like some angry spirit. And then, as quickly as it had begun, it abruptly ceased, and the old man resumed his painful progress.

'*I talk to the trees, but they don't listen to me . . .*' The words of the refrain drifted amusingly in and out of Sam's brain, but despite ample layers beneath a heavy coat, he shivered.

Inside, it felt warmer – a heavy, stuffy warmth that would have been stifling on any other day. He stood in the grubby hallway, staring at a wooden hatch with 'Porter's Lodge' written beneath it. There was no sign of any human activity, apart from the drone of a TV racing commentator coming from somewhere behind the hatch. He rapped on the plywood and in response, albeit not immediately, a beetle-browed man with a stubbly chin and a miserable countenance emerged wreathed in a cloud of stale cigarette smoke. Flicking his head up, the porter arched his eyebrows in a sullen, questioning gesture. Sam, who despised boorishness, imagined himself as an anxious relative being greeted by this paragon of affability and already felt himself getting angry. His back up, he introduced himself and unashamedly 'pulled rank'. The porter's demeanour altered reluctantly but perceptibly and Sam was directed back out of the building and towards a row of Nissen huts connected by a corridor to a single-storey brick building.

Maple Ward had no padlock on the door or bars on the windows, and the charge nurse who introduced himself as Howard had a beard and wore corduroy jeans and a baggy sweater. Sam naturally said nothing at all about Phipps's connection with Jo. Instead, he introduced himself as Ned Whelan, produced the letters he'd copied and explained his presence by telling Howard of his recent trip abroad and of how he'd heard of Dorian Phipps's relapse on his return. It was accepted with mild but pleasant surprise.

'We don't get many GPs that are interested,' smiled Howard, making Sam feel like a heel. 'Most of them wouldn't bat an eyelid if we closed.'

'Is that likely?' asked Sam.

'Oh, it's on the cards. They want to put this little lot' – he hooked a thumb over his shoulder – 'back into the community. I ask you.'

'You don't approve?'

'What? Put a half-trained care manager in charge of these poor beggars? Someone like Dorian wouldn't survive it. Bloody typical of pen-pushers. They have absolutely no idea.' He stopped abruptly and smiled apologetically. 'I'm sorry. Soapbox stuff. Come on, I'll take you to Dorian.'

'How is he?' asked Sam as he followed Howard along a passageway decorated with what appeared to be children's paintings.

'He's OK. We've had a difficult time stabilising him, but he's all right.'

They passed through a room where people – Sam assumed they were patients – sat about at Formica-topped tables. One, a lank-haired girl, looked up from

85

her painting, her face anxiously searching Sam's. Howard put his hand reassuringly on her shoulder and she returned to her watercolours without saying a word.

Turning a corner, he pushed open a door and stepped into a small room that contained a bed, an accompanying mock pine cabinet, a mock pine wardrobe and a television that gave out no sound but which was showing a period romance.

Phipps was sitting in a green plastic armchair with wooden armrests, staring at the TV. He took absolutely no notice of them as they entered.

'Dorian?' said Howard in a gentle, caring voice. 'There's someone here to see you.'

Phipps made no move, but Sam was sure he heard him say something.

Howard walked around so that he was between Phipps and the TV, and beckoned Sam to do the same.

'Hello, Mr Phipps,' said Sam, only barely remembering the close-cropped hair and the thin, pale face and sunken eyes.

'The Queen is Jesus mountain goat. The Jew is radiation no,' mumbled Phipps.

Sam felt sure he had misheard and said, 'Pardon' at the same time as he leant closer, only to hear Phipps continue:

'The Queen is Jesus mountain goat. The Jew is radiation no. The Queen is Jesus mountain goat. The Jew is radiation no. The Queen is Jesus mountain goat. The Jew is radiation no.'

It was more an incantation than a sentence. A chant that rose and fell in pitch and tone.

Sam turned to Howard, his brow wrinkled in confusion.

'Verbigeration,' said Howard matter-of-factly. 'Like I said, we've had some difficulty stabilising him.'

Sam turned back towards Phipps and looked into his white, emotionless face. Phipps was incapable of maintaining eye contact. He would occasionally sneak a glance at Sam but as soon as it was returned, his eyes would swivel away from Sam's as if the like poles of two magnets were being forced together. When they did meet for that transient moment, what Sam saw there made him want to swivel his own eyes away almost as quickly. It was like looking into the terrified, lost, bewildered eyes of some trapped animal.

A head appeared around the door. 'Howard, can you check Sheena's medication with me?'

Howard hesitated and looked at Sam. 'Will you be all right?' Sam nodded and Howard added, 'I'll only be a couple of minutes.'

Take your time, thought Sam. *Leave me alone with old crazy horse Dorian here. We've got a lot to talk about.* But to Howard, he merely smiled reassuringly. When he'd gone, Sam could hardly believe his luck. A cynical voice from somewhere deep in his left parietal lobe said, *Too bloody easy, Sammy boy. Watch it! Something bad is going to happen.* But he ignored it with a dismissive shrug. He was alone at last with the man who had confessed to murdering his wife and child. A class 1A lunatic. Well, so what if he was, it didn't change anything. There was too much of this bloody crap about diminished responsibility about anyway.

'Yes, I did rape and beat to death eighty-three-year-old Mrs Invalid, m'lud. Yes, she did only have seven pounds fifty in her purse. But I was driven to it by my craving for drink and watching Tales from a Nazi Death Camp *four times on my video.'*

Bullshit.

He could feel the anger building inside him again, rising and falling like the sea before a storm.

Come on, Dorian, my old China. Tell me what is going on in that arse-backwards bloody brain of yours. Was it really you that ploughed into my wife at fifty miles an hour? Did you think you were ridding the world of the Antichrist?

'Hello, Dorian,' said Sam.

'The Queen is Jesus mountain . . .'

'How are you today?'

'The Jew is radiation no. The . . .'

'Are you well?'

'. . . Queen is Jesus . . .' The chanting stopped as Phipps considered the question, but resumed again almost immediately. 'The Queen is Jesus mountain goat. The Jew is radiation no.'

'Dorian, I'm Dr Crawford. Do you remember me?' Phipps looked up momentarily, his features vague. 'The Queen is Jesus mountain . . .'

'You came to see me when you had the flu, remember?'

'The Jew is . . .'

'Perhaps you remember my wife better?' asked Sam. He was trying to stay calm, keeping his voice even.

'The Queen is Jesus mountain . . .'

Sam reached into his pocket and took out his photograph of Jo. He held it up in front of Phipps's face. 'Remember her, Dorian?' The chanting ceased abruptly. Phipps was staring at the photograph. He stared for a long time. Then he looked up at Sam and in his eyes there was what could have been the merest flicker of fear. The incantation started again, but it was more urgent this time, punctuated by anxious little pauses while he took in breaths and swallowed. Sam watched Phipps raise his hand to his head and curl a finger into his dark hair in a nervous gesture.

'You do remember her, don't you?' he asked.

'The Queen is Jesus . . .'

'Tell me what happened, Dorian,' he commanded.

'The Queen is Jesus mountain goat. The Jew is radiation no.' Phipps spoke more urgently now. 'The Queen is Jesus mountain goat. The Jew is radiation no.'

'Tell me what you said to the police, Dorian.' Sam's voice was insistent.

Phipps moaned and his chant became agitated. The one finger in his hair became three and instead of entwining, they began pulling at hanks in time to the rise and fall of his nonsensical mantra.

'Don't be frightened, Dorian. Just tell me what you said to the police.'

'The Jew is radiation no. The Queen . . .' Phipps stopped suddenly, his eyes glued to the photograph, and as Sam watched, something about him began to change. At first Sam thought it was just a trick of the light or of his own imagination, but after a few seconds there was no doubting the alteration. The slow, rhythmic rocking movements Phipps had performed sitting in his chair died away and were replaced by an alert, upright posture. He seemed to grow as his spine straightened. Gone was the gaunt, expressionless face and in its place appeared a wide, toothful grin. And there was something about that grin that sent a cold thrill of fear through Sam. The whole metamorphosis suggested that Phipps's body had been suddenly changed, as if somewhere someone had thrown a switch.

Sam glanced nervously at the door. Perhaps it hadn't been such a good idea to be left alone with Phipps after all. Perhaps he ought to get Howard back in.

'You shouldn't have come back, Sam,' barked Phipps suddenly, the grin fixed. He spoke rapidly, staccato words firing out, his eyes still on the photograph.

The loudness combined with the surprise of hearing his name made Sam start badly.

'What?' he said.

'Waiting for you, Sam,' said Phipps enigmatically and Sam saw saliva trickle down his chin in an uncontrolled stream.

'Who . . . who is waiting for me?' stammered Sam.

And slowly, Phipps turned his head away from the photograph to look at Sam. It was not an easy manoeuvre. The muscles in Phipps's neck bulged and strained like a weightlifter's. It gave Sam the strong impression of resistance. As if the body were obeying commands reluctantly. It reminded him of a refractory ventriloquist's dummy, the way the grin never left the face, the way the head turned independently of the eyes, the way the eyes swivelled after . . . And then he was looking directly into Phipps's grinning face and suddenly Sam knew that it wasn't Phipps who was talking to him. At least not the Phipps who had been in the room when he'd arrived.

The eyes in the face that stared back at him shone and burned into his own. They were full of – *God, what were they full of?* Nothing he'd ever seen before. He couldn't look away, couldn't break the hold they suddenly had over him. And he felt instantly frozen and naked in that gaze.

'Who are you?' whispered Sam.

The grin widened slightly. 'Someone who sees. Someone who saw.'

'Saw what?' breathed Sam, his mouth arid.

A dark patch appeared in the crotch of Phipps's trousers and began to spread outwards in a large circle as a string of saliva slid effortlessly down on to Phipps's chest. 'I let him tell and no one believed,' laughed the grin, the eyes boring into Sam's soul. 'The car was old, Sam. Old and ugly and white. Hate was the driver. Hate killed your wife. Hate smashed her. Hate waits for you.'

'How – how do you know about the car?' rasped Sam, his mind reeling.

The grin cackled. 'I hear everything, I see everything. Especially bad things. Bad things get through the best. He hears, he sees, but he doesn't like what he sees. He prefers not to tell what he sees. He hides inside himself. Sometimes, I make him tell. This time, I made him tell. Stupid, stupid. It was hate that killed her. Hate with an iron bar.'

'Who?' pleaded Sam. 'Tell me who.'

The grin cackled once more, the eyes shone brighter than ever. 'Waiting for you, Sam,' and the grin suddenly widened. It seemed impossible for it to be any wider but widen it did and Sam looked on in horror as Phipps's lip, already taut, split like an overripe grape. A bead of red blood trickled down on to the teeth and mingled with the spittle in an ochre rivulet.

'Alice says, ask her,' said the voice. And, abruptly, whoever or whatever had spoken to Sam disappeared. The body slumped, the facial muscles became slack once more and the eyes regressed into a guileless animalistic dance of fear.

'Alice?' asked Sam. 'Alice?'

Phipps threw Sam a wild, wide-eyed bovine stare and suddenly thrust both himself and the chair backwards. The noise of the chair legs against the hard floor was like a hundred blackboard chalks. Sam's hand went up to his ears involuntarily. It was just as well, because Phipps, who had leaped up and was staring at Sam as if he had recently emerged from the Black Lagoon, started screaming. If scream was the proper term to describe what was emanating from Phipps. Sam had never heard the like before. They were terrifying, unearthly, high-pitched arias that filled the whole room and threatened to pierce his eardrums.

Phipps had backed into a corner and was standing with his back against the wall, on tiptoes in an effort to get himself as far away from Sam as possible. He looked as if he were physically trying to meld in with the wall. His mouth had become an open cavern of noise, and his eyes, in complete contrast to a few minutes before, were locked on Sam's face in an unblinking, horror-filled glare.

Within seconds, although to Sam, whose ears ached from the noise, it seemed much longer, the cacophony had brought Howard and a colleague to the door.

'What the – ?'

They took in the scene and both moved quickly to Phipps, trying to calm him, to reason with the unreasonable. Through it all, Phipps kept up his clamour and added the new dimension of banging his head against the wall with an audible and sickening regularity.

Thud . . . thud . . . thud . . .

'Stop it, Dorian!' commanded Howard to no avail.

Thud . . . thud . . . thud . . .

Sam watched, stricken, as a red spot appeared on the wall behind Phipps. The thuds took on an added squidgy consistency and Sam tasted bile at the back of his throat.

'Largactil!' shouted Howard to his companion. 'Get some bloody Largactil before he knocks himself out.'

Thud . . . thud . . . thud . . .

The nurse ran for the door and almost collided with another figure who appeared at that precise moment. They performed a mad dance as they tried to let one another pass. Eventually the new arrival was left to stare at the bedlam.

'What the hell is going on?' he yelled authoritatively, and then he saw Sam. '*You!*' he said in a voice loaded with accusation and blame.

Sam swivelled round and found himself looking directly into the dark-red, angry face of Lambourne.

Later, sitting in Lambourne's office and drinking his third cup of coffee, Sam had time to reflect on his feelings. The confrontation had shaken him badly and had left him with a feeling of unreality. Had that conversation with Phipps, the *other* Phipps really taken place, or had he imagined it? Was it only Phipps who was insane? If it really had happened, what in God's name did it all mean?

Lambourne came into the room, a reproachful look on his face. He'd been attending to Phipps for about twenty minutes.

'How is he?' asked Sam.

'Reasonable now,' said Lambourne and added, 'I hope you're satisfied.'

'If you want me to say that I feel bad about this, then I do. I'm sorry. I didn't mean for it to turn out like that.'

'Just what had you expected?' demanded Lambourne.

'I . . . I'm not sure. Certainly not that.'

'Then your irresponsibility is only outweighed by your sheer naïvety.'

'You should have let me see him before,' said Sam truculently.

'So this is all my fault?' snorted Lambourne.

'You could have been more helpful,' said Sam.

'Helpful? You're lucky I don't ring up the GMC right away. Your behaviour in this has been atrocious.'

'Phipps was the only way I had of finding out what really happened to my wife. Can't you bloody well understand that?' flared Sam.

Lambourne hesitated, biting back the rejoinder on his lips, and gave Sam a long, hard, appraising look. 'Have you ever talked to anyone about this?'

'About what?' asked Sam sullenly.

'About your wife. About what happened?'

'Of course,' said Sam dismissively.

'Really talked?'

Sam said nothing.

'Tell me what you did after they found her,' said Lambourne suddenly.

Sam hesitated, despairing over the pointlessness of it, but finally and reluctantly he began to relate his actions of the last six months. He told Lambourne of his need to escape from the city and his reasons for returning to it. When he'd finished, Lambourne said, 'As I thought. You haven't had any real, professional counselling.'

'Counselling?' said Sam scathingly. 'My wife was murdered and they don't know who did it. What the hell is there to talk about?'

'Judging by your presence here today, quite a lot I should imagine.'

'Don't start spouting on about incomplete grief reactions. I've had all that crap up to here,' sneered Sam, lifting his hand to his chin.

Lambourne ignored the acerbic tone and said, 'You are as much a victim of this crime as your wife was. I feel that perhaps you should try to understand a little more about yourself. That's all I'm suggesting.'

Sam waited, his brow lined slightly.

Lambourne took a deep breath and said, 'I know something of what happened. As his consultant, I was asked by the police to comment on Phipps's ability to perform such a crime. I know that your wife was hit by a car, and that her injuries were so bad it looked as if the car had been reversed over her as well.' He paused before continuing in a low, quiet voice: 'I also know that she had been struck about the head and abdomen, mercifully after death, with a heavy object such as a crowbar or tyre-iron.'

Sam swallowed with difficulty. The image that Lambourne's words conjured up was from his worst nightmare. It still sounded appalling, no matter how many times he heard it.

'So?' he said.

'So the police asked me if this sort of crime could have been committed by Phipps. What they were really asking me was whether or not I felt that this was the work of an unbalanced mind. I didn't think Phipps was capable of it for the following reasons. The paranoid schizophrenic *is* capable of homicide, make no mistake. But it is usually a whim killing, an unpremeditated act brought on by an acute attack of the illness. From what I was told of your wife's death, it seemed inconceivable. For example, she was found in an isolated place, probably after stopping to make a phone call. Which would mean that Phipps would have had to have followed her there. That doesn't fit the pattern. Paranoics usually kill someone they know. Nine times out of ten it's a relative. Phipps had never met your wife. And quite apart from all that, he can't drive.'

Sam stared at Lambourne. He felt as if someone had thrown a bucketful of cold water over his face. Lambourne was right, there had never been any discussions like this. The police had tiptoed around everything with the utmost discretion. An attempt, he supposed, at sparing him unnecessary details. Lambourne was the first person to have talked coldly and logically about it.

'So who could have done it?' he heard himself ask in a hoarse voice.

'This type of killing usually occurs under two sets of circumstances. The first is the opportunistic killer. The man who harbours some sort of sexual or psychopathic fantasy, who happens to be presented with a set of circumstances that allows him to fulfil it. This sort of man will probably carry a knife or some other instrument of violence in his car in readiness. The premeditation here is generalised. A prime example would be one of the child murders we seem to have had so many of lately. Usually there is abduction – and how many times does the killer turn out to be a family man with children of his own? He suppresses his fantasy under normal circumstances, you see. But there is the constant urge to fulfil it. In this sort of killing, your wife would have been a hapless victim. It could just have easily been any other woman in the wrong place at the wrong time.'

Sam tried taking a sip of coffee but spat it out again. Like the day, it was cold and bitter.

'The second set of circumstances', Lambourne proceeded, 'is the premeditated murder, the implication being that your wife was the intended victim all along. Someone followed her, caught her at the moment she was vulnerable and carried out the crime in a very thorough, cold-blooded way. Usually in premeditation, the killer is known to the victim and vice versa.'

'Why are you telling me all this?' asked Sam.

'Because if it is the first type of case that we are dealing with, we're talking about an opportunistic killer, the rogue murderer. The most difficult crime of all to solve because there is no real motive, merely happenstance.'

'And what if it's the second?' Sam asked after a short pause.

'The second type of murderer is perhaps the more dangerous. Usually he kills because of an obsessional conviction that murder is the only answer to his problems. Thank God, it's a rare type of insanity. Other

95

people, some of my colleagues among them, prefer to call it evil.'

Sam nodded, a far-away look in his eyes.

'This is something you have to accept, as you must her death,' said Lambourne. His tone had changed and he was no longer angry. He had put on a more familiar hat – that of gentle persuader. 'Chasing after poor misguided fools like Phipps is not acceptance. It can only make things worse by re-enforcing your preoccupation.'

'I still smell her perfume,' said Sam falteringly. 'I still find her magazines open showing photographs of mothers and babies. I still see her.' A painful memory prompted him to add, 'She has a twin sister who is her image. I almost made a fool of myself with her a few nights ago. How can I accept her death with all of that going on? I want to be able to understand why. Why it happened to Jo. Why?'

'I didn't know about the twin sister,' said Lambourne in reply. 'It will be harder for you than for most. But these other things you describe are normal. Normal grief reactions. Some people even see the one they've lost sitting in a favourite chair or standing in a room. It's a question of the mind being reluctant to let go.'

'But something else happened in there with Phipps today. Before you came in, before he went berserk. It was as if someone else took over. He was rational, began telling me that he'd seen the car that killed Jo. How could he possibly have known that?'

Lambourne shook his head. 'How could you possibly know that it's true?'

Sam started to protest, 'But – '

'Phipps follows things on his bicycle. Sometimes it's a car, sometimes a person. I agree, he might have been near the scene. There is just the faintest possibility that he actually saw something. But it is just as feasible that it's a question of you hearing and seeing what you want to hear and see,' suggested Lambourne.

Sam said nothing. Phipps's grinning face was etched

on his brain. How could he possibly have imagined . . .

'One of the reasons I didn't want you to see him was that he went to the police insisting on seeing you,' said Lambourne gently.

'Seeing me?'

'Yes. He was convinced he had committed the crime, but he was also insistent that they warn you.'

'About what?'

Lambourne sighed. 'By the time I picked up the pieces, it was difficult to know what he was trying to say, but the police told me that he kept saying hate. He wanted to warn you against hate.'

'That's what he said to me,' agreed Sam.

'Lucid intervals are not unknown, even in as severe a case as Phipps.'

He said 'Ask Alice,' thought Sam to himself desperately. *Alice! How the Christ could he have known about Alice?*

'No, it wasn't that. It was more, I . . . I've never seen anything like that before. It was as if someone, something else took over. I – '

'They used to think that madness was a type of possession until as recently as the last century,' said Lambourne, but there was a condescending smile on his face.

'I didn't imagine it,' said Sam vehemently.

'I don't think you're in any state to differentiate between the real or the imagined as far as your wife's death is concerned'. Lambourne spoke quietly but there was a warning tone in his voice.

There was a long silence, punctuated only by a protesting moan from an inmate somewhere deep in the bowels of the hospital.

'Should I leave this city?' asked Sam. He felt bone-achingly tired all of a sudden.

'No, you must face it. Forget Phipps. Let the police do their job, and let time do the rest.'

* * *

97

Lambourne's words, so reasonable, so full of wisdom and sound advice, echoed in Sam's head as he left Greychapel. He would try, he said to himself. He'd have to humour Debbie, but in himself, he would try and 'get over it'.

But even as he resolved to adopt Lambourne's advice, the image that had haunted him for the best part of six months replayed itself in slow motion in his brain.

A car, windows misted, lights off, stands fifteen yards from the body of a woman, spread-eagled, limbs at unnatural angles, all awry in the road.

A gear crunches.

The engine revs.

Slowly the car begins to reverse, manoeuvring, making sure of its target. It picks up speed, the engine whine growing, a banshee howl in the still night.

The car lurches backwards, then up and over as the rear wheels encounter the obstacle. Bones crack like thin ice under the weight. Up and over again as the front wheels engage. The red brake lights grin luridly as the car slews to a halt. The figure in the road has a new position, limbs twisted at unlikely angles by dragging tyres.

Suddenly there is absolute quiet. The night is pitch. The car's engine a barely perceptible hum.

A gear crunches . . .

Sam squeezed his eyes shut to rid himself of the dreadful image, but it was clearer now than it had ever been. He saw now that the car was large, ugly and white.

'*Let the police do their job, and let time do the rest,*' echoed Lambourne's voice.

Why Jo? Why in God's name Jo?

The unfairness of it all. The sheer bloody waste.

Despair, deep and dark and bottomless, suddenly threatened to overcome him. More so than at any stage in his difficult journey towards 'getting over it.'

In his car, Sam tasted the warm salt of tears trickling

into his mouth. After a long while, he found himself with his hands on the keys of the ignition.

He gunned the engine and drove away without thinking, on some autopilot course that was responding only to the need to do something to break the spell of his depression. As he stopped at a junction, automatically checking the traffic flow in readiness to pull out, his attention was caught by an abandoned car. There had been an accident the previous evening, a drunk homeward bound had ploughed into a bollard. The car had been dragged to the roadside where it sat, its offside crumpled and smashed.

As Sam stared, it appeared to his fevered brain as if the car were grinning at him, mocking him, a sickening reminder of the fact that his haunting day-dream was not that far off the mark.

Shivering, he pulled out like a teenager in a souped-up Escort and sped away.

Chapter Seven

Sam saw The car again on Sunday.

He'd awakened mercifully late and in a deliberate attempt at distracting his mind away from dwelling on what had happened the day before at Greychapel, had wallowed in a sea of newsprint for the rest of the day. He did pretty well until the evening, when, at a little after seven, he opened the door to find Debbie and Paul standing there. Paul with awkward concern written all over his face, and Debbie with that smug tranquillity which disturbed Sam so.

'Sorry to turn up unannounced, mate,' said Paul, 'but we . . . well we thought maybe something was wrong. Your phone's been engaged all day.'

'Ahhh,' said Sam. 'I knew there was something I'd forgotten to do this morning.' He'd taken it off the hook the previous evening, unable to face even the most prosaic of conversations after the débâcle with Phipps.

'We were worried about you, Sam,' said Debbie earnestly.

'I'm fine,' he said simply. 'As you can see.' And then the sheer irony of it struck home and he spluttered, 'But what about you? Should you be out?'

'There,' said Paul glaring accusingly at his wife before turning to Sam for confirmation. 'She shouldn't have come, Sam. She shouldn't be out. I did try and tell her.'

'Oh, stop fussing you two,' said Debbie with a tolerant smile. 'Today is one of my good days. You know what it's like. Tomorrow I might well feel lousy again.'

'Yeah,' said Paul exasperatedly, 'tomorrow you might be back in that bloody wheelchair.'

'Wheelchair?' repeated Sam, puzzled.

'When she's too weak to walk, yes,' said Paul hotly.

'Paul,' said Debbie reproachfully, 'you know as well as I do that it could just as well happen if I'd spent the whole of today sitting in front of the TV. I have to take it as it comes, that's all.'

'I didn't know you needed a wheelchair,' said Sam with concern. His underlying guilt resurfaced; he had done nothing about contacting Embridge.

'We didn't come here to discuss me,' said Debbie with a wave of her hand, 'we came to see how you were.'

Sam looked at her, acutely aware of the discomfort he felt under her earnest gaze. He recognised it as an after-image of the deep embarrassment he'd felt the last time he'd seen her – the night he had kissed her. He wondered if she felt anything of the same kind, but he saw no trace in her expression.

Relieved, he took them through to the lounge and gave them coffee since the only alternative was brandy and neither Paul nor Debbie drank much of it except as an after-dinner liqueur.

'So was there a reason why you took the phone off the hook?' asked Debbie.

Sam thought about it and then, reluctantly at first, recounted his visit to Phipps. He left out only Phipps's strange warning, partly out of consideration for Debbie's feelings and partly because in the cold light of day it sounded frankly bizarre. He didn't want to risk any of Paul's derision, or so he said to himself. But underneath it all, for quite another, more intangible reason which eluded him, was a deeper conviction that it was something better left unsaid.

When he'd finished, Debbie had a numb, shocked look on her face, but Paul's reaction was more caustic.

'You stupid bugger,' he said. 'You could have got yourself into all sorts of trouble.'

101

Sam resisted the temptation of reminding him of who it was who had told him about Phipps in the first place.

'You poor thing,' said Debbie. 'It must have been horrible.'

•'All my own fault. In a way it turned out to be a necessary evil. I learned a few home truths.' He saw Debbie glance at him quizzically and he added, 'I've been kidding myself about getting over Jo. I don't suppose I'll ever truly be over her. But I'm going to try harder.' He smiled at both of them reassuringly.

'Well, don't pull any more stunts like that. Come and talk to me, for God's sake,' said Paul bluntly.

Sam smiled at him. It was a less than cordial invitation, but in its own way heartfelt enough.

Mercifully, Paul's irrepressible gregariousness steered the conversation away on another tack and soon Sam found himself telling them about Chloe.

'Sam Crawford!' laughed Paul. 'Talk about a dark horse.'

'She's lovely, Sam. But I thought you and she didn't get on?'

Sam laughed at Debbie's forthrightness. 'Is that what Jo told you?'

Debbie didn't flinch. 'Well, yes.'

'To be honest, I didn't take much notice of her before. She's a very complex girl.'

'But everything's in the right place, eh Sam?' Paul's smile was straight from the Fourth Form.

'Look you two, I just owe her dinner.'

Paul ignored the explanation. 'I remember when my boss came back from interviewing her. He walked around in a daze for two days, smitten. Weren't she and Jo partners in some dressmaking thing?'

'Knitwear design,' chipped in Debbie.

'Of course,' said Sam, smiling suddenly. 'I got an earful from Jo because I laughed when she told me about it. I mean, she wasn't really a chunky-sweater person.'

Debbie laughed accusingly. 'These aren't just chunky sweaters, Sam. Her designs are incredible.'

'Jo thought they were marketable, I know that.'

'So how is she doing?' asked Paul.

'She isn't,' Sam explained. 'She didn't go through with it after what happened to Jo.'

Paul whistled. 'She was the last person to see Jo that morning.'

Sam nodded. 'Is that why you interviewed her?'

'Yeah. Routine stuff. I mean she wasn't a suspect, if that's what you're asking. Sounds like she had quite a lot to lose from what happened . . .'

'Paul,' chastised Debbie through clenched teeth.

Paul checked himself and apologised. 'Sorry.'

'It's had a pretty bad effect on her, I know that. So, any suggestions for restaurants?'

'How about that place on the City Road – the Italian pescatoria?' suggested Paul.

'The one with the Venetian façade?' offered Sam, vaguely remembering it.

'That's the one,' agreed Paul. 'A bit pricey, but very nice. My Inspector used to go there all the time. Used to recommend something called the *bucatini alla flamande*. Too bloody fancy for me mind, but book early if you're thinking of going on a weekend.'

Sam looked at Debbie for any signs of regret at the fact that Paul's gourmet aspirations stretched only as far as tandoori chicken masala, but she was smiling sweetly.

They left at nine. It was Paul's last night of nights, and he wanted to run Debbie home before he went in to work. Sam knew he should have offered to let Debbie stay longer – it wouldn't have been a great deal of trouble to run her home – but he simply couldn't face being alone with her, alone with that intense conviction that revolted him so.

Instead, he saw them out with a solemn promise that he would do something about Debbie's GP the next morning, much to Paul's approval and Debbie's scowls.

'Give our regards to Chloe,' said Paul with a leer as they left.

'And don't forget to put the phone on the hook,' laughed Debbie. 'If you still want to be unsociable, switch on the answerphone.'

His mood lifted after they'd gone. Talking about Phipps had helped. And so had talking about Chloe. He searched through the local paper and found the entertainments page. There was a new season of opera at the St David's Centre. He made a phone call to the box office and followed it up with one to Chloe.

She responded equivocally to his question as to whether or not she liked opera, but she agreed readily enough to his offer of *Madam Butterfly* on Tuesday night. They chatted comfortably for what at the time seemed like a few minutes, but which turned out to be more like twenty when Sam looked at his watch after putting the phone down.

Bad sign, Sam, losing track of time. Next thing you know you'll be enjoying yourself.

He found the answerphone at the bottom of a box under some records. It was dusty and the wires were wrapped around it in untidy coils. Paul had 'provided' it and had got one for himself too. There had been no questions asked and the price of £50 was laughable when Sam knew full well that they retailed for £100.00. 'Special deal,' was all Paul had said as he'd winked and handed it over. The 'special deal' had included an annoying gremlin which intermittently recorded messages at a fast-forward speed that rendered them completely unintelligible, but for all that it had proved a very useful tool.

He remembered hating it after Jo had died. In some odd way he had blamed it for her death. Probably because she had had to use it instead of talking to him directly. If he had been there to take the call, perhaps . . . But he knew that argument held little water and at the same time he realised that without the machine he would not have had the tape. Now, as he uncoiled the wires, it was difficult to appreciate how he had felt so strongly about a grey plastic box full of circuitry. It was only a machine after all.

But it was ironic that the last time either he or Debbie had heard Jo's voice was as a message on their respective machines. Jo had rung Debbie earlier that afternoon to discuss the furniture before finally making up her mind, but had found both her sister and her husband out that fateful day.

Sam found a tape at the bottom of the box and put a new message on it, then left it in the machine and went to bed.

A deep, untroubled sleep took him until he was awakened by the phone at somewhere around two a.m.

'Hello?' he croaked. 'Hello?'

In answer, he heard a noise that initially left his sleepy mind struggling to place it. But when it did, he was suddenly, completely and terrifyingly, awake.

Through the earpiece, he heard the noise of a car engine starting.

He turned on to his back, his eyes wide and fearful, staring at the featureless ceiling, his heart jackhammering in his chest. Slowly, as if drawn by an unseen hand, he stood on trembling legs and crept across to the window. Through it, he saw the car emerge.

A big, old, ugly car.

It crawled from beyond the flickering street light and drifted slowly to beneath his window.

In his ear he could hear the soft thrumming of the engine.

'Who . . . who is this?' he whispered into the phone.

The engine kept up its monotonous drone.

'Why are you doing this?' he demanded.

In the car, he saw the window roll down and a face, pale and oval and featureless, looked back at him. He was too far away for recognition. It could have been anybody, and yet . . . and yet there was something familiar about the way the head turned, the way it was held at a slight angle, that sent his scalp crawling.

Who? Who tilted their head like that?

In his ear, he heard the line suddenly go dead. And as he watched, the face withdrew and the car slowly drifted away and disappeared into the darkness whence it had come. He stood staring after it, his heart thudding, thighs trembling, the phone in his hand, the dialling tone loud in the complete and absolute silence of the night.

For two sleepless hours he lay in bed, his mind a maelstrom of galloping, disjointed thoughts. Twice he almost managed to clear his mental screen of disruptive graffiti only to find the featureless oval face looming in the limbo of his imagination just before sleep. On both occasions his pulse raced in an adrenaline surge of fear that yanked him back to full wakefulness.

As a child, plagued with a vivid imagination that conjured up rabid wolves and sabre-toothed, red-eyed yetis, his nightmares had often driven him into his parents' bed, where he would huddle in the protective arms, his eyes peeking warily above the sheets. When he had told Jo, she hadn't laughed or scoffed. She had merely nodded and asked quizzically:

'Weapons?'

'What?' Sam had asked.

'Your parents should have given you weapons.'

Sam had laughed. 'Poison-tipped arrows, that sort of thing?'

'Of a sort. They should have told you that wolves, especially rabid wolves, die instantly at the smell of fresh green apples.'

'Apples?'

'Or at the sight of a red racing car. Something, anything that you could always carry with you. That way it would always be there in your dream pocket.'

'Is that what you did?

Jo had smiled. 'I've slain covens of witches with Cox's orange pippins.'

In his bed, the warm memory of Jo mingling with the smell of apples, Sam finally found the comfort of unconsciousness. When he woke the next morning to a beautiful crisp sunny day, he began to wonder if he had dreamed it all. And his mind, his good strong *sane* mind, realised that it was perhaps the best way to deal with it. God, if anyone was allowed a few nightmares after the last couple of days, he was.

So nightmare it was. But it didn't stop him thinking about that tilting oval face a lot that day.

Through no fault of his own, Embridge, Debbie's GP, remained unavailable thanks to a paediatric refresher course in Birmingham he was attending. It was Tuesday before Sam managed to track him down.

'Ah Sam,' said Embridge when Sam finally got hold of him. 'Heard you were back. What can I do for you?'

'It's my sister-in-law, Deborah Scott. You've been looking after her.'

'Ah yes. Our Deborah.'

'M.E.,' prompted Sam.

'M.E.,' repeated Embridge enigmatically.

'You sound a little dubious,' said Sam. 'Are you a non-believer?'

Embridge laughed. 'Did you see the *Journal* last week? Full of letters on the subject. Truth is Sam, I don't know what to believe. The best I can say about it is that I'm keeping an open mind. I've had to because as soon as I'm convinced it's genuine, those two psychiatrists from the Maudsley throw another monkey wrench into the works by insisting it's all up top.'

'What about Debbie?'

'Well, there's no doubt that she did have some sort of viral illness four or five months ago.'

'But?'

He heard Embridge sigh. 'Sam, it could well be M.E., if

107

there is such a thing. But you must remember that Deborah was your wife's twin. It must have been a severe psychological blow when she lost Jo. I hardly need to tell *you* that.'

'So you think it's all in her mind, Andrew?'

'I'm not saying that at all,' said Embridge quickly. 'It's simply that M.E. is so bloody difficult to diagnose. No one really agrees on it. Look, the loss of her sister might well have contributed to it by making her more vulnerable to a viral infection. On the other hand, she could have slid into the symptom complex we call M.E. psychosomatically as part of her grief reaction. Either way, there's not much we can do about it, apart from letting it run its course. Twin sibling loss is a psychological minefield.'

Tell me something I don't know, Andy baby. Minefield is right. And our Debbie is crossing it like a drunk wearing size eighteen boots.

'Sam, you still there?'

'Yes, I'm here.'

'You know as well as I do that there are other elements in all of this,' said Embridge quietly.

'Like?'

'Like her infertility for example. This illness she now has is a useful psychological crutch. A good reason for not getting pregnant. A good reason for not even trying any more. M.E. is an ideal disease for avoiding stress. Even minor activity can cause exhaustion.'

'You'll be back in that bloody wheelchair,' Sam heard Paul's voice saying. To Embridge he said, 'Would you mind if I repeated a few tests?'

'Delighted, Sam,' said Embridge. 'Only too delighted.'

Sam put the phone down feeling disquieted. There were question marks hanging over M.E., he knew that. But it was so unlike Debbie.

He laughed suddenly at the sentiment his own mind had thrown up like a clay pigeon ready for blasting. He came across it daily in his patients and it never ceased to irritate him.

108

'But I've never been ill in my life, Doctor,' they protested, challenging him to explain away that gem of illogic. As if a previous good health record was some sort of permanent insurance against disease.

It wasn't.

Debbie's ill, OK. All you have to do is find out whether she's genuinely got M.E., or whether she just thinks she's got it. It's what you do, Doctor, isn't it?

So why did he feel so uncomfortable about her? He knew the answer even before the question appeared in his mind. It was her total conviction, her absolute certainty that she was right, and that soon he, Sam, would know and understand that conviction too. He stared at the photograph of Jo on his desk. They were so alike, so very much alike.

Come on, Sam. Come on.

Debbie is ill – fact.

Phipps is a crazy – fact.

Jo is dead – fact.

He looked again at the photograph – a set piece she'd posed for when they'd returned home from a holiday with a few frames left in the camera. She stood outside their house with the beech hedge as a verdant backdrop, looking tanned in a bright orange T-shirt.

'Ah Jo,' he said softly. 'What are we going to do about your little sister?'

Madam Butterfly was marvellous, as was the pub on Wednesday night and *The Fisher King* on Thursday evening. Chloe's tastes were as eclectic as Sam's.

She was not an opera buff, but the English version of *Butterfly* made the story easy to follow and the music transcended language. At the end, she cried openly, apologising from behind her handkerchief.

'I had no idea it could be so moving,' she said in the car later.

'It's a pretty strong story-line,' said Sam.

'I thought you were meant just to listen to the music?'

109

Sam shook his head. 'The music is just the half of it.'

Chloe shrugged. 'I suppose I've been put off by hearing all those unintelligible arias in Russian and Italian. They sound incredibly daunting.'

'You hear people saying that there's only Italian opera. They're the same people who look down their noses at wines that don't have the right labels, despite the fact they might taste wonderful. The geniuses who wrote operas did so so that they would be heard by as many people as possible. The words as well as the music.' Abruptly, Sam checked himself and made a face. 'God, I'm beginning to sound as pretentious as the prats I'm criticising.'

Chloe shook her head. 'No you're not. I understand exactly what you're saying. The whole is so much better than the individual parts.'

Sam grinned. 'The corollary being that some parts might not reflect the whole.' He paused before adding, 'Like you, for example.'

'Me?'

Sam nodded. 'You shy away from emotion, but underneath there's a boiling sea of it.'

Chloe reddened and looked down. 'Emotion can be a dangerous thing if you can't control it.'

'It can also boil over unless it's given an outlet.'

He waited for her reply, but she turned and stared out of the window as the night traffic drifted by under the yellow street lights.

She cried at the end of *The Fisher King* as well. This time, irritated with herself, she headed for the ladies until things had dried up and the majority of the audience had left.

In the auditorium, she was the one who ended the silence between them.

'Next time promise me you'll choose something a little lighter, like *Naked Gun*, OK?'

Sam laughed. 'Don't be embarrassed. I do it all the time. The spaghetti song from *Lady and the Tramp* is guaranteed to get me blubbing.'

110

'Really?'

'Every time.'

Chloe's eyes narrowed and a sceptical smile played over her lips, but Sam kept a straight face as they made their way to a nearby pub. Over a drink and in the relaxed atmosphere of a comfortable booth, Sam found himself opening up to Chloe. She was a sympathetic listener. Inexplicably, the conversation came round to Phipps. Chloe listened, horror-struck, as Sam told her of his visit.

'I read about it when it happened. The press were horrible.'

'He's a strange man. I can't help feeling he may have seen something, but it's so mixed up with the other stuff in his head, it's hopeless.'

She was looking into his face, her eyes penetrating. 'It must be so hard for you. You must have loved her so much.'

Sam took an awkward swallow of his beer. 'Letting her rest is the most difficult thing I've ever had to do.'

'She loved you, Sam. You could see it in her eyes whenever she spoke of you.'

Sam smiled. 'You're a nice lady, Miss Jesson. A very nice lady.'

He realised suddenly that he felt good in her company. They had progresed to a stage where discussion of Jo was open and almost pain-free. And the more he was allowed to learn of the woman Chloe really was, the more he saw the qualities that Jo too must have seen. He began to realise that behind the diffident façade there was fierce loyalty and a sensuous nature. What was lacking, if anything, was happiness. Perhaps that was partly what had motivated Jo to organise the partnership. A wish to see Chloe happy.

It was a difficult thing to analyse, happiness. In fact, Sam knew that the analysis was fruitless. Work out why you were miserable or sad by all means, but happiness was simply something to be embraced unquestioningly when it came.

His suggestion of the pescatoria for dinner on Saturday evening was met with wholehearted approval. There was no reason to assume that it would not be another good evening.

No reason at all, *then*.

He went to see Debbie on Friday evening while Chloe attempted to improve herself at a word-processing evening class. Paul answered the door and ushered Sam upstairs. Debbie was in bed, looking pale and weak.

'How long have you been here?' asked Sam, horrified.

'Since Monday,' answered Paul by proxy. 'I knew that visiting you would be too much for her.'

'Debbie,' said Sam, 'how do you feel?'

'I'm fine, don't listen to Paul. I've been up today for a few hours. It's on the wane. I'll be fine by Sunday.'

She looked anything but fine. Her face was pasty and her eyes dark-rimmed.

'I talked to Embridge. He doesn't mind me running a few tests. I've come to play vampire so that I can drop the blood off at the infirmary on my way home.'

Debbie nodded wanly.

Paul left them while Sam did his venepuncture. Despite his size and bravado, Paul fainted at the merest glimpse of a needle, even when it was entering someone else's arm. Debbie chatted through it in a mildly nervous way, quizzing Sam about Chloe. 'I'm going to have to meet her, you know,' she said as he took out the needle.

'There'll be plenty of time for that.'

'It's a long-term thing, then?' she asked teasingly.

Sam smiled noncommittally and said, 'It's a shame you're not feeling well, we could have made it a foursome tomorrow night.'

'Oh, I wouldn't inflict Paul on you. He'd be looking around to see who had the biggest portion and asking for extra chips. He's a complete philistine when it comes to food.'

'You take it easy over the weekend,' said Sam warningly. 'Let Paul spoil you.'

She smiled gratefully. 'He'll be like an old hen clucking about the place.'

'Debbie, was it really coming to see me that caused this relapse?' asked Sam seriously as he squirted dark-red blood into two clear plastic tubes and began labelling them.

Debbie didn't reply immediately; she seemed more interested in a loose thread on the duvet.

'Debbie, was it?' he persisted.

'I don't know Sam. I . . . I don't think so. It's just that I'm feeling so depressed.'

Sam put down the bottle and sat on the bed next to her. 'This will all go away one day, I'm sure of that.'

'Oh Sam, it's not the illness, not directly. I've come to terms with the ME. It's you. I'm depressed because you don't believe me. You think I'm mad, don't you? You think I'm obsessed with Jo.'

'Debbie,' admonished Sam.

'Sam, please don't patronise me. Don't you understand? I wish that I didn't feel this way. That I wasn't getting the buzz. That I could forget about Jo, let her rest. That's what I want, Sam. That's what she wants, too. I thought by now she would have left you some sign,' she said miserably.

Memories of the magazines and the perfume mingled in Sam's mind momentarily with the faceless wraith in the white car, but he shook his head, shaking off the veil of confusion.

'I'm scared, Sam. Scared of what's happening to me. Is it always going to be like this? Am I going to be plagued for the rest of my life? And there are other things, too.'

'Other things?'

'Sometimes, I find myself downstairs, dressed. Sometimes . . . sometimes as if I've been outside. And I feel exhausted. Absolutely shattered, but I can't for the life of me remember what I've been doing. Those are the times I get really scared, Sam. Those are the times I feel as if I'm really going mad.'

'Debbie,' said Sam, taking her hand, 'this ME is a strange disease. The "E" stands for encephalomyelitis. It can have all sorts of strange effects on the brain.'

'Sam, I don't imagine any of these things.'

'Of course you don't. They're as real as day and night to you. But it's a trick that the virus is playing. I'll get these tests done. There's a chap in Birmingham who has a special interest in ME. If things don't improve in a day or two, I'll send you up to see him, OK?'

'Thanks, Sam. I'm so glad you're back,' she said, sinking back into the pillow and closing her eyes.

Sam saw that the effort of the conversation had been great for her. The change in her had both surprised and worried him. Not just her physical appearance, but her attitude. Gone was the fiery conviction of the zealot, and in its place was the real fear of a scared, bewildered girl confronted with the inexplicable. She was almost a different person. Her admission of the memory lapses, the fact that she was willing to concede to the faint possibility that this obsession with Jo might be psychological instead of psychic – it all argued for some sort of radical change in her. Could it be that her obviously weakened physical state had weakened her spirit too? The change he welcomed, but the implications he didn't.

Having changed once, what was to stop her reverting to the old convictions? The smiling, smug, secretive awareness she wore like a shield and which Sam despised. He wished he knew more about her disease. He knew it could produce bizarre symptoms, but . . .

'Everything all right?' asked Paul poking his head around the door.

'Fine,' said Sam. 'Just finishing.'

Paul followed him downstairs and offered him the customary drink, but Sam declined. He really did want to get the samples dropped off before the lab closed.

'Right, not to worry. I'll have yours.' He tried to make it sound light-hearted, but it merely made Sam wonder who he was trying to kid.

As Sam opened the door to let himself out, Paul exclaimed, 'Oh Jesus, I nearly forgot. Deb would have killed me.'

'Forgot what?' asked Sam.

'Next Tuesday night. Deb wants you and Chloe to come over for supper.'

Sam was dubious. 'Do you think she'll be up to it?'

'Oh, don't you worry. I've seen her like this before. She'll be fine by Sunday. She always is.'

Sam started to protest, but Paul intervened. 'Look, I know you're the bloody doctor, but I've been through this weekly for the last five months. She'll be fine. And anyway, I'm not supposed to take no for an answer.'

'I'll ask Chloe,' said Sam reluctantly.

Paul's schoolboy grin returned. 'You two a definite item then, are you?'

'Scott, shut up.'

'Hey, who could blame you, Sam? She's a real looker. I dug out her file again last week for a peek at her photograph.'

'Really?'

'Well actually it was for Deb. She wanted a reminder. Funny how they never really hit it off when Jo and Chloe were such mates. Did Jo tell you about any hold-up in this partnership thing of theirs?'

Sam shook his head. 'Was there one?'

Paul shrugged indifferently. 'Just something Debbie said the other day.'

'If she comes to dinner, you can ask her yourself.'

'Water under the bridge, Sammy boy. Water under the bridge. So, I'll get a couple of crates in. Nearly finished the bloody home-brew, you know. Yes, it'll be good to relax, have a few beers.' An oddly unpleasant ghost of a smile crept across Paul's face. Sam saw it and asked:

115

'Things all right at work?'

'Work?' repeated Paul distractedly. 'Work's fine. Work is where I escape to.' The unpleasant smile widened into an attempt at reassurance that looked about as genuine as plastic grass.

'Listen, Paul, if you ever want that drink we talked about . . .'

Paul's eyes squeezed shut as if Sam's words had triggered a spasm of pain deep inside him.

'Thanks, Sam,' he said with an effort. 'I've thought about it more than once.'

'Just pick up the phone,' added Sam earnestly. 'We can meet in that pub of yours. What's it called, The Feathers?'

Paul looked up, scanning Sam's eyes uneasily. The grin was still pasted on his face. After a long pause, he said in a strained voice, 'That's just it. I'm spending too much time there as it is.'

Sam read the chapter and a half that lay between Paul's simple lines and asked, 'How much is too much?'

'Every lunchtime a few beers. The odd five or six whiskies before I come home.'

'I can help. If you'll let me.'

Paul made a noise that might have been meant as a laugh. 'Don't know if I want help, Sam. That's the trouble.'

Sam waited for him to continue. Upstairs, he heard Debbie shifting about in her bed. When Paul spoke again it was in a low croak laden with guilt and misery. 'In the pub, I get what I can't at home. It's a good crack, a laugh. Shit, at least I can talk to people there. Here, we don't talk about anything any more, Sam. Debbie and I are strangers.' His eyes suddenly became haunted. 'The thing is, I've begun to look at some of the girls there . . . I never used to look at any before. Never needed to . . .'

'Things will work out, Paul.' Sam prayed he sounded convincing.

'You think so?'

'Yes, I do.'

A thin smile, genuine this time, crossed Paul's jowly face. 'What a mess, eh?' he managed, and Sam heard a touch of the old laugh in it.

'You must try and ride it out, Paul. She may not even know it herself, but Debbie needs you.'

Paul sighed and nodded. When he spoke again, he made an effort at lightness.

'OK, Sammy. See you Tuesday with the delectable Chloe. Just hope I can make it, that's all. They found a tart strangled in Adamstown last night. Looks like I'll be in for some overtime next week. That's what I mean, Sam. Work is just fine.'

Chapter Eight

On Saturday morning, Sam drove around the Bay, the huge dockland area that was currently being redeveloped along with countless other seaside cities whose ports were no longer economically viable. Even his own flat was in a converted warehouse in an area rather grandly called Atlantic Wharf, a few hundred yards from where a huge flyover had sprung up to ferry people to the new leisure complexes that were part of the great 'plan'. The view from the flat by day was hardly inspiring: wide expanses of marshland rolling towards the shoreline, here and there dotted with grimy container depots and the hulks of abandoned factories that sat like forgotten callouses on the skin of a beached whale. As he drove across the wasteland, he could see that the developers were moving in, like laughing hyenas on the fringe of a kill. A gleaming new County Hall dominated one end of the huge expanse of emptiness. It sat, forlorn despite its pristine condition, waiting for the private sector to cast a cosmetically acceptable spell over the neighbouring desolation and decrepitude. To the west, Butetown and the docks waited slyly to see if Tiger Bay could really be transmogrified into squeaky clean, characterless, fast-food Yuppymarinaville.

But it hadn't happened yet. Driving down James Street was still like jump-jetting through three continents. You were as likely to meet a Somalian as you were a world-weary whore. And strangely, that pleased Sam. He was discomfited by the knowledge that his nostalgia for the place was probably ill-founded

118

sentimentality, but at least the place was alive and had character. God save real life.

When he got back, he tidied up the flat and went for a run. It was after he emerged from the shower, his skin pink and glistening from the hot water, that he noticed the small red light glowing on the answerphone. He rewound the tape and turned the volume right up so that he could listen while he shaved. After the usual staccato clicks and whirrs of connection, what came over was nothing more than a series of high-pitched blips that lasted about half a minute. Then the connection broke and the blips gave way to the hiss of empty tape running through the heads. He rewound again and got a repeat performance. Peeved, he took the tape out and examined it, checking the housing and rattling it a few times, even rotating the spool with a pencil to check for tightness, but it ran freely enough and seemed perfectly normal.

It could be the machine again, of course, he thought to himself, but being the pragmatist he believed himself to be, he did the simplest thing first and exchanged the tape, leaving the suspect one on top of the machine, where he promptly forgot all about it.

That evening he picked Chloe up from her house, an unpretentious semi on the expensive side of one of the city's lake-filled parks. They had a drink in a wine bar that, despite its distance from the city centre and an anticipated quietness, they were lucky to get a seat in. They talked about foreign cities and travel and Sam found himself envious of the way Chloe nonchalantly ticked off the many places she had seen.

'New York,' he said wistfully. 'It's the one city I've always wanted to visit. Never got round to it and now I have misgivings about going there alone.' He spoke honestly, not angling for sympathy.

'I know what you mean. Its reputation does go a little before it. But it's really no worse than any other big city. What you need is a streetwise guide. Someone worldly-wise. Like me.'

'Worth seeing then?'

She smiled beatifically. 'Taking off from Kennedy at night with a high cloud base, the whole city stretches out before you. You can almost reach out and touch the World Trade Center. It's indescribable.'

'You still miss it, the flying I mean?'

'Sometimes, only sometimes.'

The restaurant, when they got there, had changed hands. The name had remained but the new owners had turned it into a bistro of sorts. Instead of Verdi, it was Piaf who provided the background music and the menu was chalked up on a blackboard. Orders were taken by a chef behind a cold counter where the meat and fish were displayed, and the mainly chargrilled dishes were brought to the table by vaguely Mediterranean-looking waiters. Sam's first reaction was to apologise, but it was obvious that the place was doing a roaring trade and by implication could not be *that* bad, and Chloe generously said as much. They sat at a table illuminated by a yellow candle stuck into the neck of a rosé bottle that had been emptied of its original contents at least a year ago, judging by the amount of melted wax that was cascading over the faded label. The place was a little too loud, a little too full and could have done with a little bit less in the way of lighting in Sam's opinion. But he realised that his expectations had been geared towards a more intimate evening and it brought a rueful smile to his face.

'Private joke?' asked Chloe, seeing it.

'Not quite what I was expecting, that's all,' he said.

Chloe cupped her chin in her hands with elbows on the table and said, 'Let's have a glass of wine and see how we feel. It looks like it could be fun.'

On his way back from the men's room, Sam found himself saying hello to a couple of people in the cramped space between tables. Both were doctors, one another GP and the other a consultant at the University Hospital. Both were with their wives, and both had 'Lucky sod' written all over their faces as they saw who

Sam was with. It was hello and goodbye with the GP, but the consultant insisted on discussing a patient Sam had referred earlier in the week.

'Sorry,' he said to Chloe as he sat down again. 'Old Lipincott is a bit intense.'

'Don't worry, I daresay I'll get used to it – ' She stopped in mid-sentence, a look of dawning horror spreading over her face as she realised exactly what had emerged so spontaneously from her lips. 'I . . . I . . .' she stammered.

'I know what you mean,' said Sam, laughing.

'Oh God,' she said, squeezing her eyes shut. 'I think I'd better have some more wine.'

Sam replenished both their glasses, his eyes wrinkling in amusement, and wondered why her *faux pas* had triggered such a strange excitement inside him.

They both agreed on prawns in a garlic sauce and a tossed green salad.

Noise buzzed around them, and waiters squeezed by with trays laden with food, but Sam hardly noticed any of it. He was happy just to be there, to be able to talk and to laugh and not feel guilty any more. To be normal.

It was after their second cup of coffee that it happened. So quickly that it was only later, in the cold light of retrospection, that he realised he'd seen the man standing at the bar, watching them. But since Chloe drew stares like dentists drew teeth, it hadn't made much impression on him at the time.

The waiter had just refilled the coffee cups and Sam was in the middle of pouring cream when he heard, in a loud, theatrical voice, *'There you are!* My God, how can you just sit there?' Conversation dropped instantly from roar to flicker before sputtering into silence, and Sam saw heads turning as people tried to locate the voice.

'How can you do this to us? Don't you care anything at all about the kids?'

The voice was one of desperation, of a man at the end of his tether. A begging, beseeching voice. Sam pushed back his chair and craned his neck in an attempt to see. It was coming from somewhere behind him, from a man in his late thirties with hollow cheeks and a forehead creased in a permanent frown of worry. He was only a couple of feet behind Sam, his hands held out in a gesture of hopeless pleading. But it wasn't until he spoke that Sam realised that he was looking at, and talking to, Chloe.

'What happened to you?' asked the man wretchedly. 'What did I do? Whatever it was, I'm sorry. But please *please* come back, for the kids' sake. I'll move out, I'll do anything, only please don't keep doing this to us.'

Sam's eyes swivelled round to look at Chloe. She seemed paralysed, her eyes unblinking and wide, her face a frozen mask of horror. He saw her mouth shape itself into the semblance of a quivering question. 'Who. . . ?' she whispered.

'Chloe, for God's sake, at least say something to me now I'm here. Don't pretend that you don't even know me,' moaned the man.

For what seemed an age, Chloe's eyes were locked on those of the interloper's, but then, with an effort, she managed to break away and look at Sam. He saw her swallow and shake her head in denial. At the edge of his vision, Sam could see that everyone within range had turned to stare. Even the waiters had paused to enjoy the spectacle. Nothing like a bit of dirty washing being hung out in public to titillate the masses, he thought angrily.

He swung round in his seat and stood up to confront their visitor.

'Who are you?' he asked.

The man laughed, throwing his head back in a humourless cackle. 'You mean she hasn't told you about me? About the husband and children she ran out on? Well, well, I wonder why.' He spat out the words, literally. Sam felt a wet pinprick on his cheek and blinked involuntarily. He turned back to Chloe. She

122

seemed dumbstruck, and as he watched he saw her face turn from crimson to a deathly white.

'OK,' said Sam, standing up, 'I don't know who you are, but I think you'd better leave.'

In response, the man coughed. A raking, chest-burning, rasping rattle that made him lean on an adjacent chair for support. Sam could only watch helplessly. Finally, he wiped his mouth with the back of his hand and stared at Sam defiantly.

'If I was strong enough I'd knock your bloody teeth in,' he said. 'But I don't want to end up in hospital over her again. Someone has to look after the kids.' He turned back to Chloe, his mouth a sardonic grimace. 'She knows where to find us – don't you?' He swung his arm up and pointed a final accusing finger at her before stalking out. He almost made it to the door before another bout of coughing took him and he faltered, leaning weakly against the wall until it passed.

Like the curtain falling on the first act, noise and bustle recommenced almost immediately on his exit. Sam sat down, bemused by the episode. Out of the corner of his eye, he saw the barman smile and shake his head slightly. It seemed an incongruous gesture, very much at odds with the pointed looks they were getting from every other part of the room.

Chloe's eyes were fixed on her lap, and Sam saw that she was trembling.

'Do you want some more coffee?' he asked ineffectually.

She looked up, her eyes huge and frightened, her lips compressed into a pale tight line, as if opening them might allow some terrible emotion to escape. Finally, she managed to shake her head. Sam looked over to an adjacent table where a portly woman with a hard unsmiling face was staring stonily at Chloe. He'd been unfortunate enough to have suffered the ordeal of having to listen to smatterings of her conversation all evening. She had done nothing but complain about the food, the wine, the service and life in general since she'd lowered herself into her chair. He watched as she stuffed a forkful of cheesecake into her mouth and said to her long-suffering partner:

'Bloody bitch. Ought to be bloody shot.'

'Come on,' said Sam to Chloe, loudly enough for the fat woman to hear. 'Let's go before I throw up.' He laid three twenty-pound notes on the table and ushered Chloe outside without a backward glance. They didn't speak until they were in the car. Sam put the key into the ignition, but hesitated before starting up. Instead, he turned to Chloe and asked, 'You OK?'

She nodded mechanically, but kept her eyes straight ahead.

'If it's any consolation,' he went on, 'I didn't believe a word of it.'

She jerked around to stare at him and he saw that she was still quivering with emotion.

'That was . . . horrible . . .' she said, her voice unsteady. 'Wuh . . . why would anybody do that?'

Sam shook his head. 'You didn't know him then?'

'I've never seen him before in my life. And those people in the restaurant . . . The things they said about me. They don't even *know* me,' she said entreatingly.

Sam sat with the wheel in his hands. There was something bothering him. Something quite apart from the actual attack on Chloe's character. The barman! Yes, the barman's reaction had been strange to say the least. That resigned smile and the shake of the head. As if he'd seen it all before, as if it were something that happened all the –

'Wait here,' he said, getting out of the car.

'Where are you going?' asked Chloe in a small, frightened voice.

'I'll just be a second,' he said and walked back towards the restaurant. When he came back five minutes later, he found Chloe in the same hunched-up position in her seat, clutching herself, shivering.

'You either have some very, very misguided friends, or at least one malignant enemy in Cardiff,' he said as he swung into his seat.

Chloe stared at him. Her face, which had been a picture of tortured misery, suddenly sharpened inquisitively.

'What?'

'You've just had a nastygram.'

'A what?'

'A nastygram. As your vociferous visitor left, I saw the barman's reaction. It was as if he'd just heard a favourite joke all over again. It looked as if it was familiar to him. I was right, he had seen it all before. And he also said that we'd had the maestro performing it.'

'Performing what? Who was that man?'

'A nastygram. That was the nastygram man.'

She shook her head, exasperated, and Sam explained. 'It's a modification of a kissogram. They also do strippograms and gorillagrams, apparently. The barman said that usually at the end the chap gives the victim a note explaining who sent him. He was very surprised to hear that you didn't get one. It's all designed to cause maximum embarrassment to the victim. Worked pretty well too, didn't it?'

'My God,' said Chloe, disbelievingly. 'It made me feel sick, physically sick.'

'Like the man said, he was one of the best.'

'But who . . .'

Sam held up his hands.

Chloe nodded. 'You're right. Only very good friends or a really vicious enemy would do something like that. Especially without leaving a note.' And she laughed. A nervous chuckle that grew into a gut-aching, tear-spilling howl as she pictured the scene as it would have appeared to everyone in the restaurant. A scarlet, heartless tart who had abandoned her kids caught in an adulterous act and forced to listen to the outpourings of her hard-done-by husband. Sam watched in amusement until at last the gales abated into intermittent giggles.

'Thank you,' she gasped, 'thank you for going back.' She leaned over and kissed him. And what began as a simple peck of gratitude accelerated like a runaway train into something much, much more urgent. They sat in the car, hunched over like hungry teenagers, passion overriding their discomfort until Chloe, her eyes heavy lidded, her mouth still moist and open, said, 'Let's go home, Sam. Home to bed.'

Any apprehension that Sam had harboured about his capability, or even his desire, for lovemaking after Jo, evaporated instantly in Chloe's king-size bed. She seemed as hungry for him as he was for her and her energy galvanised him. Their first coupling was a frenetic, feral coition, driven by primal lust. But the second, which was indistinguishable and seemed to flow on from the first, was a slower, more sensuous voyage of pleasurable discovery. The way Chloe commanded and encouraged him to probe and caress her with his mouth heightened his own excitement. Once again he was struck by the discrepancy between the face she presented to what she perceived as a hostile world and the real passion of her desire. Strangely, he had almost come to expect it. Certainly, in her bed, he revelled in it. She, in turn, was driven to more than one exploding orgasm as she gave herself up to the soft meanderings of Sam's tongue and the teasing strength of his fingers.

Finally, at two a.m., Chloe unwrapped her long legs from around Sam and they got up. Sam sipped wine and munched tuna-covered crackers as, entwined in each other's arms on a voluminous settee, they talked. Sam sensed that this part of sex – 'the afterglow' Jo used to call it – was just as important to Chloe as the act itself. They had that much in common at least.

They discussed the débâcle in the restaurant, but even after racking her brains, Chloe could come up with no one who could have thought of such a malicious stunt.

'It's creepy,' she said.

'It's been a creepy week altogether,' sighed Sam reflectively.

Chloe turned her face up to his inquisitively.

And slowly, waveringly at first, Sam told her about smelling Jo's perfume and the magazines in his flat. His voice became low and tense as he described the oval face that haunted him, the words seeming to flow out of him as he stared at the pale-gold liquid swirling in his glass like a fortune-teller looking for answers in the dregs of a teacup. Finally it was all out, even his concern over Debbie. Chloe listened with a mixture of incredulity and sympathy, stroking his hair as he unburdened himself upon her.

'Oh God, Sam. I had no idea,' she said when he'd finished. 'It must have been hellish. Your sister-in-law sounds . . . troubled. Strangely, I don't know much about her. Jo was oddly reluctant to talk. A problem like that is the last thing you need after what you've been through. I mean, what can *you* do for her? Is there anything?'

'Physically, probably not. But I'm beginning to wonder if I ought to talk to Lambourne about her.'

'Why don't you?'

Sam shrugged. 'Somehow it would seem almost an act of betrayal. An abuse of her trust in me.'

Chloe was silent for a moment, but finally she said, 'Sometimes it's better that way, Sam. Sometimes your mind can play nasty tricks on you.'

Sam didn't speak. Something told him there was more to come.

'Remember I told you about having to leave the airline?'

Sam nodded.

'Well, I wasn't totally honest with you. When I said that I left the airline of my own accord, that wasn't strictly true. In fact, I had a breakdown, although that seems like a strange way to describe what actually happened. I was heavily involved with another crew member – a first officer. When we broke up, it became pretty ugly. I'm afraid he was very physical and extremely jealous. The things he tried to do to me after we'd broken up were unbelievable. I took it all for a while – until I couldn't stand it any more. Something snapped. I . . . I fought back. He ended up in hospital. Oh, not badly hurt, he needed a few stitches. I think his pride was damaged more than anything, but it did something to me, losing control like that . . . It made me ill.' She paused, composing herself for what she was about to say.

'You don't think he was the one who set you up in the restaurant?' asked Sam suddenly.

Chloe shook her head. 'It did cross my mind, but I can't see how. He lives in the States. He doesn't even know where I am.' Sam nodded, relieved. 'Anyway,' continued Chloe, 'I grounded myself and went to a psychiatric hospital for a few weeks – voluntarily, you understand – and it did me the world of good. I got a lot of help there. So I understand, you see. The point I'm trying to make is that until I lost control, I had no idea of what was really happening to me. And I know that it could have been much worse.'

'What are you trying to say?'

'I'm trying to say that the sooner you get your sister-in-law help, the better.'

'Unless, of course, what she says is true and she really is in touch with Jo.'

Chloe studied him, her face softening with pity.

'You still miss her, don't you?'

'Yes,' he said honestly, secure in the knowledge that Chloe wanted the truth.

'You must have loved her very much.'

'Everyone did.'

'Have you any photographs? I've got one we took together in the evening class.'

'Only one that I carry. But I have her voice.'

'Her voice?'

'On tape. I always carry it so that I can listen. Do you want to hear it?' he asked tentatively.

'Would I be prying if I said yes?'

Sam shook his head and smiled at her. Still wearing a towel from the bathroom and nothing else, he padded over to his jacket and took out the photograph from his wallet and the tape from its customary place in his pocket. Chloe switched on the hi-fi and he gave her the tape. She rewound it and sat down to listen expectantly.

'Hello,' said a voice from the speakers, 'I'm afraid I'm not in to take your call at present, but . . .'

'Shit,' cursed Sam. 'It's the wrong bloody tape. I must have picked this one up as I left the flat. Force of habit.' He moved to switch it off but Chloe, stifling a giggle, stopped him.

'Let's hear it all,' she said and Sam gave in with a long-suffering look. When his message was over he said to Chloe, 'Listen to this. See if you can make anything out of it,' and got up to turn the volume up so that the high-pitched squeaks that had sounded so odd that morning were audible.

'Sounds like a shoal of dolphin,' she said when it had ended.

'You're a great help,' said Sam and proceeded to explain about the answerphone as he exchanged the tape for the real one, which he retrieved from the other pocket of his jacket. They listened in silence to Jo's last words to Sam, while Chloe studied the photograph.

'She was so pretty,' said Chloe, 'and her voice is so full of her *joie de vivre*.'

'Now you know why I listen to it. Do you think it's morbid of me?'

'No,' she said firmly, handing back the photograph. 'If you'd used Jo as an excuse for not going to bed with me, I might have said yes. As it is, I can't see anything wrong

129

with cherishing her memory at all. It seems . . . only natural.'

Sam smiled at her gratefully. 'What about you?' he asked.

Chloe shook her head, sending her hair swishing. 'Nothing serious, not since . . . I've lost touch with the few male connections I had while I was flying. I wanted it that way. I needed to make a clean break. And since then I've tried to keep busy . . . Indulge myself and – ' She laughed self-consciously. 'Wait for the right person, I suppose.'

'Indulge yourself?'

Chloe hesitated before saying, 'I suppose you'd find out eventually. Love me, love my sweaters.'

She got up and padded off before returning with two large knitted sweaters of intricate design.

'Wow,' said Sam. 'You made these?'

'Designed and knitted by C. Jesson.'

Sam took one from her and stared in open admiration at the chunky jacket. Dynamic stepped patterns marched up the garment in large blocks, but on closer inspection Sam could see that each block was made up of cleverly arranged lines of colour, close enough in tone to blend and soften at a distance, but vibrant close-to.

'This is amazing,' he said genuinely.

Chloe gazed at him cynically.

'No, I mean it. My God, no wonder Jo was so excited about it. How the hell do you even begin to design something like this?'

'Easy. I take my inspiration from looking about. This one is based on some church steps I saw.'

'They must be worth a fortune.'

Chloe laughed. 'I wore this to paint the back door last week.'

Sam looked aghast. 'You're kidding.'

Chloe shrugged.

'Have you tried selling them?'

'I've sold a couple of basic designs, but what I'd really like to do is exclusive designs. Open a small shop.'

'Marketing was what Jo was going to do for you?'

'We're in a recession remember,' she said ruefully.

'But there's a market for stuff like this, isn't there? I've seen them in Covent Garden. Arm-and-a-leg jobs.'

Chloe shrugged again. 'One day, maybe.' She took the things away and came back to sit with him.

'I'm impressed. Truly.'

'I'm glad,' she said snuggling up.

'It explains a lot,' he added.

'Oh?'

'I couldn't imagine how anyone as bright as you could be content with Mr Urquart. Now I know.'

'Not many people know my little secret.'

'You should broadcast it to the world.'

'You're a nice man, Sam Crawford.'

'I'm more than that. I'd like to be your next business partner.'

'Don't be silly.'

'Why not?'

'Are you serious?'

'Of course. I have money. More than I can use. I think of it as Jo's anyway. Insurance money . . .'

Chloe looked suddenly aghast and shook her head. 'I couldn't use that money, Sam.' Her eyes filled.

'Listen to me. This is what Jo wanted. It would be a monument to her if we could make this work. Now, I'm not sure I can be as much help as Jo, but we could get help. Professional help.'

Chloe stood and paced agitatedly for a minute, her hands wringing in front of her. Finally, she stopped and knelt at the settee, clutching his hands.

'Do you really mean this?'

Sam laughed. 'Of course I mean it. I need to invest in something.'

'When you put it that way, it sounds a lot better. OK. Partner.' Sam saw a spark of excitement in her eyes.

'I'll get on to the solicitor on Monday.' He laughed.

'I'll get him to iron out the little problem that was slowing things up for you and Jo.'

Chloe frowned. 'What little problem?'

'I don't know the details. Paul mentioned it the other day. Jo said something to Debbie about it, I think.'

'I wasn't aware of any problems. Everything seemed to be going smoothly.'

Sam said uncertainly, 'Really. I just assumed . . .'

Chloe's face remained a blank page apart from two small, questioning creases between her eyebrows.

'Obviously Paul got it wrong,' conceded Sam. 'Anyway, let the legal people sort it out. In a couple of weeks we should be in business.'

A smile wiped away the creases. Her hair was held back from her face with a slide, and in the half-light of the low table lamp her eyes shone.

Sam stretched out on the settee. 'This is the most relaxed I've felt in months. Whoever it was who glued up my car that day couldn't possibly have known how big a favour they were doing me.'

Getting over it, Sammy boy.

Chloe kissed him gently on the cheek. 'Well, it was about time you got lucky, wasn't it?' She scooped up their cups and plates. 'Come on, let's go back to bed.'

They slept, showered together when they woke, made love again and had brunch at eleven. Afterwards, they strolled briskly around the lake. A morning mist had stubbornly persisted as a freezing fog that chilled the air. Sam offered to make dinner and found a delicatessen open that sold pasta and some reasonably fresh-looking basil while Chloe bought a couple of bottles of wine. Neither of them seemed in any great hurry to escape from one another's company, and the meal seemed an excellent idea.

Sam was in the kitchen in the middle of making a bolognese sauce when Chloe called to him. She'd begged his indulgence and while he was cooking had disappeared into her study to finish some letters that

132

Urquart needed doing by Monday morning. Now her disembodied voice sounded tremulous and frightened and made Sam hurry to the small boxroom on the ground floor that she had turned into a study. It was there that she kept her typewriter and her Dictaphone. She was sitting with her earphones on, her face white and streaked with tears above her trembling lips.

'What's wrong?' asked Sam.

'Your tape,' she sobbed anxiously. 'Not your wife's, I mean the one with the funny squeaks on . . . I'd . . . I'd finished my letters . . . I was playing around, I wanted to hear your voice again. Your answerphone voice was . . . you sounded so serious.' Her face cracked into a disjointed smile.

'And then I heard the squeaks . . . and I had the idea of slowing them down, like I do with Mr Urquart if I can't understand him.' She hesitated. 'I've slowed it down as much as I can. Here – ' She took off the earphones and held them out to Sam. 'You'd better listen.'

Sam set down the spoon he was still holding and put on the earphones.

'Ready?' asked Chloe, her eyes huge.

He nodded and she pressed the button that sent the tape running. He saw her knee flex slightly as she controlled the speed with her foot switch. He heard his own voice and then the squeaks as before. He nodded to Chloe and the tape started to slow so that the squeak instantly became a Pinky and Perky voice intoning a still incoherent chant. Chloe's foot pressed down so that the tape almost stopped, and suddenly the voice became comprehensible. The chant became two words. Two monosyllabic words.

A plea.

'Help me . . . help me . . . help me . . .'

But it was the other feature of the voice that froze Sam's marrow. The world swam in front of him, his mind recoiling from the information it was being forced to assimilate. He could hear his heart as it thumped and missed a beat, once . . . twice . . . He exhaled and drew in a breath. He felt a sudden dull pain in his hand and saw that he had picked up a pen from Chloe's desk and broken it in some convulsive grasp. The cut ends of the rigid plastic had dug into his palm and he saw numbly that there was blood running over his wrist.

'*Help me . . . help me . . .*' the voice continued, each utterance identical in pitch and intonation.

Sam moaned.

'*Help me . . . help me . . .*'

'Please . . .' he cried.

'*Help me . . . help me . . . help me . . .*'

'No, no, no, no . . .' He stared at Chloe and saw pity and horror and realisation written there.

She knew too. She knew from having heard the voice before, '*Help me . . . help me . . . help me . . .*'

Like Sam, she knew that it was Jo's voice.

Chapter Nine

'*Help me . . . help me . . . help –* '

The voice stopped abruptly. Sam couldn't move. His legs had turned to lead just as readily as his mind had turned into a slowly melting mound of ice cream.

'*She'll find a way,*' he heard Debbie say in a calm, assured voice. '*Don't worry, Sam, she'll find a way.*'

His brain rebelled, it simply could not be. Every rational bone in his body cried out in protest.

But it is, Sammy. It is.

Through the muffled silence of the earphones he heard a sob and looked up to see Chloe's face running with fresh tears. He saw her hand reach out and gently peel open his fingers. He felt hot tears on his palm and the blood there meandered in a new diluted stream. He felt no pain, only numbness. Like the faint buzz that plagues the ears after leaving a particularly noisy concert. Only his numbness affected all his senses.

Shock, Sammy boy. Shock from hearing your dead and buried wifey calling you on the old dog and bone. Do you think there's a queue for the kiosk over there, Sam? Do they have the same hassle with foreign operators, do you think?

He laughed. A strange high-pitched giggle that stopped only when Chloe slapped him, hard.

The next couple of hours remained a vague and hazy pea soup to Sam. He remembered only snatches: the cold air hitting his face as he left the flat, a coat being thrown over his shoulders. He had no idea how long he spent outside, but Chloe was with him when sensation –

and no other word could better describe the return of his awareness when it did eventually come – reinstated itself in his consciousness and the mental fog lifted.

They were sitting on a bench in a park – Chloe's park – and the overriding feeling he had was one of bone-aching cold. His hands were blue and he felt something mucoid and wet dripping tantalisingly from the tip of his nose. He couldn't feel his toes, and his lips, when he tried to move them, felt as though they had come fresh from a marathon session with a needle-happy dentist.

Chloe's head disentangled itself from his shoulders and she looked up at him. Her eyes were skittery and red-raw from the cold, her face a bloodless ivory. She was shivering, despite the layers she had wrapped herself in. He noticed vaguely that the mist still hung in the gathering gloom of the evening.

'You must be frozen,' he said finally.

Chloe started, surprised at hearing his voice, but before she could reply, Sam's eyes dropped to the black pavement and he began in a stilted monotone to tell her about Alice. It seemed to emerge from him unbidden. Driven out like an exorcised demon.

Chloe listened, numb from the cold and from the horror of it, her eyes never leaving his face.

After a long cold silence, she asked: 'What made you think about Alice?'

Sam mumbled: 'Jo's voice . . . All I could think about was Phipps. His face changing in front of me. His lips splitting into that other . . . thing. The thing that knew . . .' He paused, letting out a cloud of steaming exhalation before he added in a papery whisper, 'I thought I heard Phipps tell me to ask Alice . . .'

'Oh, Sam,' said Chloe concernedly, squeezing his arm tightly. They were both silent for a while, a silence broken only by their chattering teeth.

'How long have we been out here?' Sam asked eventually, lifting his eyes from the floor.

'An hour and a half,' said Chloe shivering violently.

'I'm sorry,' he said. 'Why didn't you go back inside?'

'I was scared to. Scared to leave you alone. I didn't know what you were going to do . . . I . . .'

'What did I do?' he asked candidly.

'You walked around the park. Three times. We've been sitting here for half an hour.'

'I was thinking of Alice,' he said dully.

Chloe nodded understandingly and led him inside. Neither of them could move very quickly, their limbs were stiff and unresponsive. As Chloe soaked in a bath, Sam stood under a hot shower that ran for at least half an hour, his hands turning from blue to angry, agonisingly painful purple and finally to a tingling red. After hot chocolate and brandy, he announced that he wanted to listen to the tape again. Chloe didn't try to stop him but he could see that she doubted the wisdom of it.

She's scared you're going to do another Mr Hyde on her, Sammy.

'I'll be OK this time, really,' he said and hoped to God he was right. But the smile she gave him in return was full of misgivings.

This time he worked the foot pedal himself and she watched pensively as he listened, his face grim. When he'd finished, he sat at Chloe's desk repeatedly removing and replacing the click-on top of a felt-tip pen.

'It is her, isn't it?' asked Chloe. But it was more a statement that required confirmation than a question.

'Yes, it's her.'

'But how. . . ?'

Sam laughed mirthlessly.

'Sam, don't. It isn't funny. When I was in the hospital . . . I met people who believed all sorts of things. That they were saints, or could see things, or . . . much, much worse. That was why they were in the unit. And some . . . some believed that they could talk to the dead. But it can't really happen, can it?'

The Queen is Jesus mountain goat . . .

'It already has,' said Sam, looking at the tape.

137

'But what does it mean?'

'It means I ought to crawl back to Debbie on my hands and knees and beg forgiveness for doubting.'

The memory of the perfume and the magazines in the flat resurfaced in a new light. Could they have been real? Not something he'd imagined or done himself? You read about this sort of thing all the time. Surely there was a grain of truth in some of it? And Jo and Debbie had had this thing between them, there was no doubting that. Perhaps it really did provide a link, a door that had been left ajar.

What about Lourdes, Sammy? Thousands of people believe in Lourdes. And what, if you boil it down, is that all about? A ghost. Some little girl out in a grotto sees a ghost and Bob's your uncle. And boy oh boy, do people believe in that little poltergeist. Ask the lady who's still there after good old Doc Badnews took one look at the secondaries in her left lung and gave her six months to see the world, ten years ago! *Some bloody ghost!*

It suddenly seemed possible, all so possible.

His mind was abruptly frozen by the fragment of a thought that wafted into his brain like poisonous gas on a treacherous breeze. A jumbled collage of torn memories and snatches of conversations that burst like an electric charge into his head. But, tantalisingly, their significance eluded meaning and they faded instantly into nothing more than an uneasy feeling akin to a vivid *déjà vu.*

'Sam?' said Chloe concernedly. The vague, fragmented apprehension he'd experienced earlier tried to burst through again, but it was swamped by the new-found conviction he had that Jo had been trying to get to him.

Chloe pulled the towelling robe she was wearing around herself protectively and walked around the desk to stand near Sam. She looked like a child.

'Sam,' she said, 'I'm scared.'

Sam stood up and held her. He knew that he needed

the comfort of her embrace as much, if not more, than she needed his at that moment.

He spent the night with her, neither wanting to be alone. But it was a very different night to the previous one. This was a sexless, broken night during which they clung to each other for comfort, not passion. Sam was spared the Alice dream. Instead, he dreamed that something, some red-eyed *thing*, had crawled under his bed and was lying in wait. It was a terror drawn from his childhood, a combination of all his demons, the regression effortless. The *thing* was biding its time, lying in anticipation of someone daring to peek under the bed and glance into its wild, maniacal eyes. Eyes that flashed with fearful glee.

The Queen is Jesus mountain goat . . .

In his dream, Sam saw the *thing* melt and change into a recognisable form. A vague, human form that lay curled under his bed, clutching a box he realised was an answerphone, its wires hanging like the entrails of a small animal. The figure, he saw, was wearing a mask. The mask was a grotesque Scarfeian caricature of Dorian Phipps.

Sam played out Monday like a dazed actor in a terrible play. It was like trying to function through a blanket of cotton wool. He recognised the feeling; it had been much the same after Jo's death. It was an emotional reaction in its truest sense. Having suffered a severe emotional jolt, he had become a non-sentient being. His feelings had gone into cold storage. He functioned on some other level; an automaton, still capable of decision-making but with an absence of any real humanitarian response.

What was worse were the thoughts that rode a carousel inside his head. Jo and Debbie and Chloe and Phipps were the riders that kept bobbing up insistently on dumb, blind horses. But he had no answers to the questions they posed. So they kept riding, going round and around.

The worried, anxious stares he met on the faces of his colleagues said, '*Poor Sam, it's all proving too much for him. He's cracking up. We knew it would come. Poor old Sam.*'

He tried to fix a reassuring smile on his face, but it felt like the photograph he always remembered from a musty textbook: a man in the middle of a tetanic seizure, his face dragged up by the muscle spasms into a risus sardonicus. And yet, that morning, lying awake at dawn in Chloe's bed, they had both decided that work was the answer to the day's problems.

Work would distract the mind.

Except Sam's mind wouldn't listen.

His only consolation that morning was that at least he had decided what was to be done. He would speak to Debbie. She would know what to do. She had to know.

When he'd told Chloe that morning, she had shivered, but hadn't objected. She had merely made him promise to come back to her that evening. A plea rather than an invitation to spend another night. He suddenly felt a rush of feeling towards her. A mixture of gratitude for her support and guilt at the way he was embroiling her in his troubles. She didn't deserve any of it. Especially after what she'd been through. God knows, she'd had troubles enough of her own. Her psyche must have taken a pummelling after the breakup, and the destruction of her partnership would undoubtedly have compounded the grief of Jo's death. She was in no position to offer guidance as to which road to take in this strange land he was travelling. He felt pleased that he had decided to help with financing her business. It felt right somehow. If anything good came out of all of this, it would be a miracle.

So he would speak to Debbie.

Alone.

He phoned her at lunchtime and arranged to go round at five; it would be safe then. Paul would still be at work – the busy murder enquiry demanded compulsory overtime. Debbie seemed eager, as if she could sense something in his voice. But he said nothing over the phone. After fixing the meeting, he felt better. At least it was something. Something positive.

He sat at his desk, his eyes straying to a well-thumbed Yellow Pages sitting on a shelf. On impulse, he picked it up and found five entries under Telegrams and Greetings. He picked up the phone and dialled the number of the first entry: Adonis Kiss-o-Grams. The girl who answered recited a little rhyme that made Sam cringe. When she'd finished, he cleared his throat and asked if they ever insulted people.

No, came the reply, they didn't do nastygrams, but they did a service called Long-lost Sister, or Brother, which was almost the same thing – and much cheaper. Yes, she did know which company did nastygrams, but she was sure he'd find their service much better *actually*, and – '

Sam cut her off in mid-pitch by saying that he was ringing up to complain, *actually*.

The malicious glee with which she provided the guilty firm's name and number spoke of a fairly tense rivalry. It was an unusual name – The Camel's Back – but clever, and very apposite he had to admit. He wrote it down in his diary, right underneath where he'd written Lucy Kendrick's name.

Sam stared at it. For a long moment it stared back at him blankly.

Who the hell was Lucy Kendrick?

And then the image of the girl Ned Whelan had arranged one of his 'late' appointments for crystallised in his memory.

Commendable conscientiousness on the part of Ned, had it not been for the ulterior motive Chloe had made Sam aware of. Frowning, Sam realised that he had hardly thought of Ned in days. Neither his name nor his face had featured in any of the chaotic happenings that had turned Sam's world upside down. He stared again at

Lucy Kendrick's name written in his own hand and felt the germ of a sick, unpleasant idea take root and twist itself like icy fingers around his gut.

Debbie was waiting for him. The first thing he noticed as he walked through the front door was a wheelchair, folded, leaning against a wall in the kitchen. He threw her a troubled glance.

'I'm fine today,' she said. 'A bit rough yesterday, that's all.'

He winced, remembering again Paul's prediction when he and Debbie had visited him.

'Paul's being kept pretty busy,' she said conversationally.

'I expect a murder enquiry is quite intensive.'

'Usually,' she agreed, and there was a reticence in her voice that made Sam sit up.

'What is it?'

'He's been over at Greychapel all day.'

'Greychapel?'

Debbie nodded distastefully. 'Phipps is dead.'

Sam stared at her in stunned silence. It was a full minute before he managed to croak, 'How?'

'An accident of some sort. He was knocked off his bicycle.'

Sam shook his head. 'Oh Christ.'

He sat down in the living room, suddenly acutely aware of the pocket of silence that enfolded them. He didn't know where to start.

'You sounded . . . funny on the phone,' ventured Debbie.

Hys-fucking-sterical, I'm sure, he thought, but said: 'Debbie, on Saturday I got a phone message. A very strange phone message. It didn't sound like a message, it didn't sound like anything to start with. Until yesterday, that is . . .'

And then it all came out, like projectile vomiting. He couldn't help himself: the perfume, the magazines in the

142

flat, Chloe being insulted in the restaurant, hearing Jo's voice on the Dictaphone. His words echoed in his head and emerged from his lips stilted and strange. Insane words, like the ramblings of some crazed junkie.

But the look in Debbie's eyes when he'd finished was not that of a sceptic. The look was one of victory.

'Oh, Sam,' she breathed, her eyes shining. 'I knew it, I knew she would.'

Sam gazed at her with troubled eyes. 'I wish I had your faith, Debbie.'

'But surely you can't have any doubts? Not now. Not after she actually spoke to you?'

'I want to believe it, Debbie. I really do, but . . .'

'But what?'

Lucy Kendrick, said a voice in his head.

'Well, what does it mean, for God's sake?'

Sam saw her eyes become vague for an instant, as if she was suddenly lost in a dream, but then they cleared and focused and it left him wondering if he'd really seen it at all.

'I think I'm beginning to know what she wants, Sam,' she said.

Sam shook his head, still doubtful. 'Debbie, I don't know. This is all so bloody strange. None of it makes any sense. This attack in the restaurant really frightened Chloe.'

'But surely that was just a practical joke,' she said dimissively.

'Some joke. Usually the victim gets told who's behind it all. That didn't happen this time.'

'Perhaps he forgot. Perhaps he took one look at you and decided it was best that he left.'

Sam considered it, remembering the anger he had felt. He said grimly, 'It doesn't matter. I'm going to find out anyway. I've got some time tomorrow afternoon. I'll go to their office.'

Debbie frowned and said, 'You're tilting at windmills, Sam. Don't you think you're overreacting?'

'I have to know.'

Debbie sighed. 'Well, if you must. Don't be late for supper, that's all. And you must bring Chloe, she's part of it now. In fact, tell her to come early. It'll give us a chance to talk. We can have a girlie chat. I'll need her support as well, Sam. It'll be my vindication after all these months of waiting.'

'Waiting for what?' asked Sam expectantly.

And for an instant, he thought she was going to tell him. Her eyes suddenly blazed triumphantly, alive with fire and understanding, but she faltered and the fire went out. Instead she said haltingly, 'No . . . no, not yet. I want you there, Sam. But I want you on my side. Chloe believes, doesn't she? Paul must be made to understand.' Her eyes were full of pleading. 'I'll tell everyone tomorrow night. I want it all to be out in the open. Tomorrow night, over dinner.'

'But, Debbie – '

'No, Sam. It has to be this way. I have to be sure.'

Sam was full of misgivings. But he'd fanned the flames of Debbie's convictions and there was little he could do about that, he knew. And there was the small matter of Jo's message. *Help me . . . help me . . . help me . . . You heard it too, Sam. Loud and clear.*

Lucy Kendrick, said the new voice. It was angry and bitter and wondering how easy it might be to make sick phone calls . . .

'I won't be late,' he promised.

His doubts about involving Chloe still further multiplied as the evening wore on. *She* had no qualms about going to Debbie's for supper, he knew that. The qualms were all his, and they were tied up with his own tormenting difficulty in accepting the improbable. That was a direct result of several nebulous factors, not the least of which was his medical training. His daily life was tied up with science. An explanation for everything had been his watchword.

It's 1992, for crying out loud, his brain kept protesting. But was that enough to preclude the possibility of the paranormal? He knew that for some people, the twentieth century and all its technology meant nothing. In the newspaper that very morning he'd read a paragraph that had staggered him. In Turin, a city where the motor car was a god, if not the God, where car manufacturing expertise was supposed to be amongst the most advanced in the world, he'd read that the city's bishop had increased the number of priests he employed as exorcists to four. *Four*!

He also knew that not so long ago, a piece of information like that would have brought a cynical smile to his lips and he would have clicked his tongue and shaken his head sadly. But now, he simply didn't know what to make of any of it any more.

The events of the last couple of weeks played and replayed themselves in his brain. Yet what bothered him more was Phipps's death. He rang Paul at work and eventually received his return call an hour later. He was less than effusive when Sam pressed him for details, his voice exhausted from too many cigarettes.

'Tricky, Sam. It's an ongoing, see.'

'Oh come on, Paul. I visit the guy and only days later he's dead. What the hell is going on?'

'Hey Sam, calm down. Nothing is going on.'

'So how did it happen?'

Paul sighed. 'Old Dorian rode his bike everywhere, Sam. He hardly ever walked. Someone ploughed into him near the back entrance of the hospital. It's quieter. He liked to ride around there.'

'Christ. Anyone else hurt?'

Paul hesitated. 'No. We don't think so.'

'What do you mean, you don't think so? Don't you fucking know?'

'Come on, Sam, lighten up.' Paul's sigh echoed over the line before he added reluctantly, 'The fact is . . . it's a hit-and-run. We don't know who the driver was. It was late, getting dark . . .'

'And no one saw anything?'

'A hint of a colour.'

Silence hissed while Sam tried to swallow.

'What colour?'

'Pale. Yellow or white . . . We aren't sure.'

'Jesus. Jesus.'

'Sam, what's the matter?'

'Something bad is going on here, Paul. Something very bad.'

'Hit-and-runs happen all the time. It doesn't mean shit. It doesn't mean it's connected in any way, Sam.'

Sam laughed mirthlessly. 'Crap, Paul. One hundred per cent crap. Of course it's connected. It's all connected.'

'Why would anyone want to get rid of Phipps now, for Christ's sake?'

'Because I'm back. Because I showed an interest.'

'Oh great, Sam. So now you're blaming yourself for Phipps being run over? That's a good one. That's a cracker.'

'It's not only that. There are other things.'

'What other things? Tell me.'

Sam checked himself. His mind whirled. He needed time to think. Time to work things out.

'I will tell you. But not yet. Not just yet.'

'Sam? . . . Sam?'

He hard Paul's voice yelling as he put down the phone.

Despite pushing Chloe to think really hard again, she still could not come up with anyone who might have wanted to set her up in the restaurant, and that bothered Sam greatly. She sat in her living room, legs drawn up under herself, sipping coffee. 'I don't think I've ever been so embarrassed in my life. Embarrassed and scared,' she added with a little shiver.

'Embarrassment is a powerful tool,' said Sam

distantly. Chloe looked at him oddly. He took the cup she offered and qualified his statement. 'It's almost a social disease in this country. Look at the lengths we go to avoid it.'

'Well, I would have done anything to have avoided that.'

'Always assuming that it was aimed at you,' said Sam abruptly. Chloe frowned. 'What do you mean?'

'What if you weren't the real victim? What if you were merely the pawn?'

'I don't follow.'

'What if I was the one who had the very good friend –'

'Or the malignant enemy,' said Chloe nodding, finally catching Sam's drift.

But Sam was too busy thinking about his car. About it being glued up. About how *almost* everyone had been glad to see him come back to work. About Chloe's reason for coming to see him as a patient in the first place.

There was someone mean and petty enough to use Chloe as a victim of his dirty tricks. The more he thought of it, the more convinced he became and the more anger he felt simmering away inside him. Without realising it, his mind welcomed the anger, fed on it, revelled in it. It was a channel for the emotional energy that had been building up since hearing Jo's plea. It glowed and fizzled inside him like a lighted bomb that was targeted in one direction and one direction only. For that reason, it was a dangerous anger. Not because of its volatility, but because it was welcome and thus distracting.

Alone and hapless in the forest of his confusion, Sam saw only the trees. And the woods became completely obscured from view.

Chapter Ten

Sam's anger simmered through the morning clinic. He didn't see any of the partners during the course of it and felt perhaps it was just as well. He left promptly after his last patient with a cursory nod to Brenda, anxious to get on with what he was determined to do.

The day was clear and crisp, a welcome change from the soggy depression that had hung over the city for the last few days. But already he could see dark clouds building to the west and the respite looked as if it might be short-lived.

It was after two by the time he had located the address. It stood in an arcade near the castle, above a leather boutique full of spiked heels and studded jackets. A weasel-featured salesgirl eyed him suspiciously as he pushed through the side-door adjacent to where she lounged, black-painted lips in continuous disdainful motion as she chewed on some gum.

The man who sat behind the desk at The Camel's Back wore mascara and a blue plastic badge that announced his name as Robert. The room was small by any standards, but was made oppressive by the decoration that stood out in three dimensions. There must have been a hundred masks stuck to the walls, all hollow-eyed and threatening. Sam recognised a few of the parodies of the classical Greek faces of tragedy and comedy, but others were surreal or overtly horrific. They smiled or grimaced down at him, mocking and silent.

Robert appeared to be busy with some paperwork and

when he did eventually look up, it was with the indifference of someone who tolerated intrusion as part of the job, but who relished it not one iota.

'Yes?' said Robert disinterestedly.

'A friend of mine recommended you to me,' said Sam. 'One of your people did a little act at a party. My friend's boss was the target. He pretended they'd spent the night together after being picked up in a pub. It was very good. I, uh, wondered if I could hire the same chap?'

'It was a man then?'

Sam nodded.

'Did you know his name?'

'Unfortunately not, but I'd recognise him.'

'We have four boys who do nastygrams,' said Robert, reaching underneath the desk for a portfolio. 'Three of them are actors, and the fourth is a student. Have a look.' He opened the folder and pushed it across to Sam.

The photographs were stuck to the top right-hand corners of four sheets of typed paper. Two were unflattering passport black-and-whites, the remaining two colour glossies in soft focus. Sam had no difficulty recognising Chloe's visitor from one of the latter, although the clean-shaven man who stared out at him bore little resemblance to the haggard consumptive who had verbally assailed Chloe.

'That's Jeremy,' said Robert, twisting his neck round to look at the page. 'The best, and the most expensive.'

'How much?' asked Sam.

'Anything up to a hundred. Depends on what you want him to do.' Robert's eyes flicked down and up Sam's coat.

'I did speak to another company called Adonis Kiss-o-Grams. They said they were cheaper than – '

'There is *no* comparison,' said Robert derisively. An attitude that suited him admirably. 'Jeremy is a professional actor. He's done loads of TV. He was in that cider commercial last year. The one with Robin Hood in Sherwood Forest.'

Sam nodded, trying to look suitably impressed. 'Still, it's a lot of money. I'm not sure if I can convince the other people who want to hire him. I wonder . . .'

Robert's eyebrows rose enquiringly.

'Does he work lunchtimes? If he did, I could take the others round to where he was performing and they could see for themselves how good he was.'

Robert shook his head. 'Sorry, he works evenings only. He's usually busy auditioning during the day. Forever over at the BBC or HTV. Anyway, we're not supposed to divulge information to anyone outside of the client about where or when a nastygram is taking place.'

Sam nodded understandingly and smiled sadly at Robert. 'That's a shame. I'm sure they'd want him if they could see what he can do. And this woman they want to set up is such a bitch.' He sighed.

Whether it was his smile or his misogynous attitude that changed Robert's mind, Sam was never sure, but change his mind he did.

'They'd kill me if they found out,' he said in a conspiratorial tone, 'but I know he's doing something tonight in a pub. The Book and Candle in Canton. If it was a private party, I wouldn't have told you. But since it's in a pub, you could just happen to be there at the same time . . .'

'Thank you,' said Sam, smiling.

'It's an after-work thing, about sixish. And don't say I never did anything for you,' said Robert fluttering his dark-blue eyelashes outrageously. 'And you'd better come back and see me about the booking, OK?'

Sam held the smile until he was out of the door and then dropped it from his face like a wet rag.

He drove to the Book and Candle and bought himself a pint of bitter topped with lemonade, deliberately choosing a drink he hated so that he wouldn't imbibe it too quickly. He sat in a corner watching the afternoon trade drift in and out, mulling over the information he

150

had gleaned, pleased at finding Jeremy but at the same time disappointed at not being able to get at him immediately. But then, he rationalised, it was the bastard behind it all that he really wanted to get hold of.

The angry voice still simmered inside him. A voice that wouldn't go away.

Why bother with the monkey, Sammy, when you know who the organ-grinder is?

But did he? Did he really know?

Of course you do. Forget the actor. Go and see the malicious bastard who put him up to it.

The thought wouldn't leave him alone.

Why bother with the monkey, Sammy?

It stoked the fire of his burning anger.

Why bother . . .

Sam left the sickly beer and drove back to the practice. He hung around, pushing paper around his desk until the noise from the waiting room had finally abated. At five, he stuck his head outside the door and saw Brenda behind the desk as usual.

'Hello,' she said. 'I thought it was your afternoon off?'

'Couple of things I need to sort out. I'm surprised to see you still here,' said Sam.

'Dr Whelan's got one patient in with him and one to come. I'll hang on for another fifteen minutes.'

'Don't bother. I'm going to be here for a while longer. You get off.'

Brenda's face lit up. 'Oh, Dr Crawford, you are an angel. You're sure you don't mind?' she asked, her coat already half on.

'Off you go.' He held the door open for her and watched her trot to her car. He walked around to sit behind the desk and, after a couple of minutes, saw Ned Whelan's door open and a girl emerge and start walking towards him. He stood up as she approached and heard her say:

'Oh, has the receptionist gone?'

'Yes,' said Sam. 'Can I help?'

She looked anxious and a little scared as she clutched

her appointment card tightly. 'Dr Whelan wants to see me again on Friday,' she said resignedly.

'Right,' said Sam cheerfully and turned the pages of the appointments book.

'Can you make it about the same time,' she said. 'Dr Whelan says it's much more convenient for him at this time.'

Sam looked up dubiously and held out his hand for her appointment card, studying her name. 'Ah,' he said. 'Friday. Now didn't Dr Whelan say something about Friday? Hang on a second.' He took out his diary and studied it. Only the slight pursing of his lips betrayed any emotion, but as he looked up his face wore a beatific smile. 'No, I was wrong. Friday is fine.'

He made as if to write her name down in the book. 'You're becoming one of our regular visitors, aren't you, Ms Kendrick? We'll have to get you an armchair with your name on it.'

'Oh, I hope not,' she said earnestly, and glancing over her shoulder guiltily, she asked, 'Is there any way you could ring the hospital and ask them to make sure my result is back before Friday? I would have asked Dr Whelan, but he's such a busy man. I know it's very kind of him to see me like this . . . it's just that I want to know about my test.'

Sam stopped pretending to write in the book. He hadn't written anything because he had no intention of booking her in again. Lucy Kendrick had gone through enough, as her presence in his diary attested.

'Your smear test you mean?' he asked.

'Yes,' she replied awkwardly.

'Do you know,' he said, as if the thought had just occurred to him, 'your name is very familiar. Do you have a moment? I have a funny feeling that I may have seen your result somewhere.'

'Really?' said Lucy Kendrick hopefully.

Sam ushered her into the coffee room and gave her a cup from the dispensing machine outside.

Ned Whelan's face registered an instant of surprise before regressing to its usual belligerence as Sam walked in without knocking.

'Do you mind?' he said acidly. 'I'm in the middle of a clinic. And anyway, is knocking on doors a capital offence in Australia?'

'Why? Have you got something to hide?'

Whelan eyed Sam coolly before asking, 'What exactly do you want?'

'An answer to a question.'

Whelan sighed. 'It's late, Crawford. Too late for playing silly games.'

'Too right,' said Sam with feeling. 'Tell me why you're bringing that girl back to see you again.'

'Which girl?'

'Lucy Kendrick. The girl who was in here two minutes ago.'

'What the hell has that got to do with you?' said Whelan, his small eyes hardening.

'How many times has she been back now? Three is it? Or perhaps four?'

Whelan looked as if he was about to spit, but then he changed his mind and sat back in his chair with elaborate slowness, his lips compressing into a thin smile. 'OK, I'll tell you why. She's awaiting a smear test result.'

'Then why haven't you given the lab a ring?'

'What the hell for? It'll come in its own sweet time. Ringing up the lab every two minutes doesn't engender a good working relationship.'

'That is pure unadulterated crap, and you know it,' said Sam. 'That girl is worried sick.'

'She's got nothing to worry about,' sneered Whelan dismissively.

'How do you know that?' snapped Sam.

'Because – ' began Whelan, but checked himself and retorted, 'this is none of your bloody business anyway.'

Sam stared at him coldly. 'You were about to say, because she's negative, weren't you?'

'How could I? I haven't – '

Sam moved so quickly that Whelan had no time to react. He yanked at the drawer of Whelan's desk. There was a crack of snapping wood as the retaining catch gave and it came out in his hands like a reluctant baby.

'That's private,' yelled Whelan.

'No it isn't, its practice property.' Sam put the drawer and its contents down on the examination couch as Whelan stood up and came round the desk towards him.

'Sit down, Ned,' said Sam calmly. There was something in his voice that momentarily stopped Whelan in his tracks, but then he recovered and came forward again, his face as black as thunder, his arms raised menacingly. He flailed a fist towards Sam which missed its main target but caught him a glancing blow on the temple.

Sam hit him low down. Like the shock wave in front of an express train, Whelan's breath hissed outwards as his face went from purple to pale green in five seconds flat. Sam manhandled him back into a chair and left him gasping for air as he turned back to the drawer.

They were exactly where he remembered them to be – under a stone paperweight in the far left-hand corner. There were four of them in all. Lucy Kendrick's was the third in the pile.

He swung round to Whelan, who was clutching his abdomen and making high-pitched noises in his throat. 'You bastard,' said Sam and barely restrained himself from hitting him a second time.

'You . . . you've ruptured something,' wheezed Whelan.

'Don't tempt me,' said Sam in disgust and added, 'Why?' as he held up the smear results. 'Tell me why?'

Whelan turned his pale face away and said nothing.

'OK, save it for the FPC. I hope you've got a good lawyer.'

Sam started towards the door and it was only a faintly whispered 'No . . .' from Whelan that stopped him.

A trace of colour had returned to his face, but to Sam he suddenly looked very old and somehow smaller and pathetic. 'My wife and I . . . we don't get on. Haven't done for years. We no longer live together. I haven't done anything wrong here, Sam,' he pleaded. 'These women . . .' He pointed at the results in Sam's hands. 'Half of them give you the come-on anyway. You know that.'

'What?' said Sam in disbelief.

'Oh, come off it, you know they do. All I've done is given them the opportunity. I don't do any of the pushing.'

'And how many of them have ripped your clothes off so far?' Sam's sarcasm was almost lost amidst the anger in his voice.

'There've been one or two,' said Whelan quickly. A little too quickly.

'You liar,' hissed Sam. 'You lousy, pathetic liar. These women came to you for help. Jesus Christ! I can't believe you could do this. You must have caused untold damage.'

'I don't do it if the test is positive,' whined Whelan.

'You rodent. I don't believe you. I wouldn't believe you if you told me that the sun was going to rise tomorrow. I think you're capable of anything.'

'How . . . how did you know?'

'I just had to use my eyes and ears.'

'Who?'

'Don't pretend. I found her result in the same drawer six months ago. You almost had a fit when you saw her sitting outside my room three weeks ago.'

'Jesson,' whispered Whelan.

'Yes, Jesson. Ten out of ten. Christ, that must have irked you. That really must have pissed you off. So much so that you had to exact some sort of juvenile revenge, right? Did it please you to pour glue into the locks of my car? Not half as much as trying to make Chloe Jesson look like a heartless bitch in front of me, I bet.'

155

'What. . . ?' said Whelan.

'Don't come the bloody innocent.' Sam felt his breath coming thick and fast. 'Chloe knew. She knew, and you know what I've been thinking? I've been playing the "What if?" game. What if Chloe knew and told her friend. Her friend who just happened to be married to another member of the practice. You know what I think she'd do? She would confront you. Because she was that type of person. She wouldn't waste any time on discussion. She would root out the bad apple.'

Ned continued to stare, the beginning of a very worried frown dragging at his eyes.

Sam's voice held an icy calm now. 'Is that what happened, Ned? Did Jo come and tell you to get your act together or say goodbye to your pension? Is that why you waited for her outside the phone box?' Sam felt his teeth grind together and spittle start to fly. 'Wait in that stupid fucking shitty fucking car of yours so that you could run her fucking over?'

Ned wasn't simply staring now. His eyes had become craters of fear.

'Sam, for God's sake wait. Look, I'll admit that I did bring some of these women back unnecessarily, and I promise I won't do it again. But this stuff about glue in your car and making your girlfriend look bad in front of you – and Jo.' He was shaking his head rapidly from side to side. 'That's madness, Sam. I don't know anything at all about that. Jo never came to see me. Never.'

Sam wanted to hit him then, he wanted to see blood. He hadn't despised anything or anyone in his life as much as he despised Whelan at that moment, but he forced himself to stay as calm as he could. 'Are you telling me that you didn't put superglue in my car the afternoon that you found Chloe waiting to see me?'

Whelan, his eyes wide and desperate, shook his hed.

'And it wasn't you who paid the actor to play the deserted husband the other night, or sent me a sick message on my answerphone?'

Again Whelan shook his head. 'Sam, this is strange stuff you're spouting here. I swear I had nothing to do with it. I swear on my mother's grave.'

'And it wasn't you who killed Jo?'

Ned was shaking his head.

'ANSWER THE FUCKING QUESTION!'

Ned jumped. He jumped so hard that he lost a glassful of urine from his bladder. He began pleading with Sam.

'No! I swear to God, no. No. No.'

Sam's focus came back with a jolt. He had lost himself there for a moment. But as he watched the cringing man in front of him, he suddenly became silent. He had been so sure that it had been Whelan. So absolutely certain that only Whelan was capable of such vindictive, murderous acts. But the frightened, snivelling rodent before him seemed suddenly incapable of anything as . . . passionate. Sam balked mentally at the word that had sprung to mind. But it was what he was searching for. If someone had deliberately killed Jo, they must have felt an overwhelming emotion. A passionate hate, or love. Whelan, Sam realised, was totally impotent on that score.

So if it isn't Ned, then who is it? And more important than that Sammy boy, why?

Whelan took in Sam's reaction and ventured to gain a little ground. 'Does that mean that you and the Jesson girl are – ?' Sam threw him a glance full of red flashing danger signals. Whelan saw it and held up his hands in apology. 'Only asking, Sam. Only asking.' He paused, and out of the corner of his eye, Sam could see Whelan's weasel face light up as he thought of something else.

'The Jesson girl,' said Whelan, 'there was something odd about her, wasn't there? Not physically, I mean. Far from it. But wasn't there some trouble, something about a breakdown?'

'OK, Ned. Get your two penn'orth in. She had a mild breakdown, yes. It's exactly the sort of thing you would bloody remember.'

'Mild breakdown,' scoffed Whelan. 'That's not how I heard it.'

'What do you mean?' asked Sam suspiciously. He still didn't trust Whelan an inch.

'There were letters in the notes passed on to me from her last GP when she joined the practice. Usually letters tell only half the story, so I rang up the hospital. I wanted to know what sort of a lunatic I was dealing with. The chap I spoke to there said she nearly killed some guy. A pilot I think he was. For no reason at all, apparently. Just completely blew her top. She was only a hair's breadth away from being sectioned.'

Sam stared at him with distaste. 'You make me sick,' he said. 'And it sounds like whoever you spoke to has the same exceedingly high standards of confidentiality that you have. Or is this more bullshit, Ned? Because if it is, I might just have to hit you again to make you shut up.'

'It's food for thought, that's all,' said Whelan quickly.

'In what way?'

'Look, I don't know how intimate you and Miss Jesson are. It just strikes me as odd that all these things happen to you after meeting her, that's all. And knowing her background for what it is. I mean, this business in the restaurant sounds bloody bizarre, but I bet it didn't work, did it? I bet you ended up giving her all the sympathy, right?'

Yes, how did it turn out, Sammy? Didn't you end up going back to her place for a game of doctors and nurses?

Shut up.

And what about the car? Convenient that Chloe should be passing at just the right moment, wasn't it?

Shut up.

And then there were the magazines, and the . . .

Shut up.

Shut up.

SHUT UP.

'*Shut up!*'

'OK, OK, Sam. I'm sorry, OK?'

Sam had unknowingly moved forward and was leaning over Whelan, his fists curled into tight balls, his teeth clamped together under drawn-back lips.

He had almost lost control then.

Almost.

He moved back, wiping saliva from the corners of his mouth with the back of his hand.

Whelan watched him with large, saucer eyes. 'What are you going to do?' he asked after a moment.

Sam said nothing. His mind was still on the whirligig that Whelan's words had set in motion.

'Sam? What are you going to do about the results?'

'Shut up, Ned.'

'But Sam?' wailed Whelan.

'If I ever see a woman near this room after five again . . .' Sam tried to make it sound menacing, but it was hopeless. He couldn't think. He couldn't even be bothered to hate Whelan any more.

'Thanks, Sam. Thanks. You're a real pal.'

Sam left. Ned's voice was beginning to make him feel sick. He found Lucy Kendrick and gave her the result, barely noticing her gratitude and relief. He left her standing in the doorway of the surgery, a bemused look on her face as she watched him run to his car.

Probably an emergency, she thought.

And she was right. It was after six.

Jeremy had already begun his act at the Book and Candle.

Chapter Eleven

Jeremy was in the middle of his performance when Sam got to the pub. He found the bar virtually deserted and for one desperate moment thought he'd missed it. But obligingly and in reply to his question, the landlord pointed him in the direction of a back room with a cursory, 'They're in there.'

Sam nodded gratefully and found the room – somewhat grandly called the 'Games Room' – which was full of young men in shiny suits standing elbow to elbow with flat-chested girls with Burberrys slung over their arms. Over in a corner, near a pool table, an older man was standing and staring at Jeremy, who had perched himself provocatively on the edge of the green baize. Sam's view, over one man's shoulder and between the heads of two girls, was patchy. But he could hear everything since, like him, most of the people in the room were straining to listen too. In fact, they were lapping up the act and their faces showed expectation and delight at the victim's bewilderment. Jeremy's role seemed to be that of injured boyfriend. As Sam watched and listened, he felt there was something terribly familiar about Jeremy's characterisation, but he couldn't quite put his finger on it.

'Is it because you don't think I'm good enough for your friends? Is that it?' asked Jeremy in his clear actor's voice. It was not an overtly effeminate voice, but there was enough in it to leave one in no doubt as to the meaning behind such a loaded question. The intonation, the ringed fingers and the preening hands sent out even

160

broader signals. And then Sam realised that it was Robert he was looking at and listening to. Jeremy had needed to go no further than The Camel's Back office to find his role model.

The victim's bewilderment, bordering on desperation, suddenly inflamed into anger. 'Look, you little queer,' he retorted, 'if you don't bugger off, I'll – '

'It's no good pretending, Charlie, I'm not going to disappear in a puff of smoke.' Jeremy was playing to the crowd.

Someone giggled and it broke the spell. Sam watched Charlie look up suddenly, try to catch the eye of one of his colleagues, but fail as the colleague shied away from eye contact.

Instantly, Sam saw Charlie's expression change from disbelief to one of appreciative acknowledgement. He knew he was being had. The moment was a true test of character, and Charlie rose to it well.

'Oh all right,' he said to Jeremy. 'You can stay. But I'm not putting those handcuffs on again. Not until later, anyway.'

The crowd roared with approval as Jeremy rolled his eyes dramatically.

Everyone began talking at once, clapping Charles on the back, toasting him, enjoying the big joke. Jeremy had played him like a big fish so that everyone could have their fun, keeping the line taut until it started to look ugly. Then, and with consummate ease, Sam realised, he'd let him slip off the hook.

Unlike Chloe.

Jeremy suddenly stood up and took something from beneath the pool table. It was a gift-wrapped parcel, which he duly began to present to Charles. Robert disappeared and in his place stood Jeremy – or at least the Jeremy who was used for presenting gifts. He'd done his homework well, Sam could see that. His speech was peppered with silly innuendoes and in-jokes that the audience revelled in. As a final twist, he gave

Charles a peck on the cheek. He was good, Sam had to admit.

It was all so very different to what had happened in the restaurant. This was fun because it had never been allowed to become hurtful or distasteful. Jeremy was in absolute control. Sam watched as he took his applause and one or two curtain calls. He stood in the doorway, out of sight, amazed at how two of the girls were flirting outrageously with the actor. One of them invited him to stay on and join them for a meal later, but Sam heard him refuse politely.

'Duty calls,' he said with a shrug.

Sam turned his face to the wall as Jeremy left the room. He followed him as far as the toilet and sat on a stool in the bar to wait for him.

When Jeremy emerged, Robert had been left behind in a sinkful of inky mascara. His boyish face looked stark and just washed, and his hair was different and slightly damp. He carried a small sports bag and wore a long khaki trench coat in the style that was currently fashionable.

Sam grabbed his elbow as he passed. 'Nice performance,' he said.

Jeremy, surprised but not troubled by the physical contact, turned and smiled broadly after only a moment's hesitation. 'Thank you. Always helps if the audience is appreciative.'

Sam nodded. 'Drink?'

'No thanks,' said Jeremy. 'I'm a bit pushed for time.'

'Is it interesting work?' asked Sam.

Jeremy laughed. 'Different anyway.'

'But you enjoy it?'

'Pays the rent.'

'Are you sure you don't want a drink?'

'Certain.'

'It's just that I find business easier to discuss over a drink,' persisted Sam.

Jeremy tilted his head appraisingly. 'Business?'

162

'What would you like?'

Jeremy shrugged and sat down. He ordered an orange juice. 'What sort of business had you in mind?' he asked.

'Nothing too demanding – for a man with your talent. Be like falling off a log for you.' Sam kept his voice even and hoped his smile seemed genuine.

'Oh?'

'A bit of private work. I want to embarrass somebody. Publicly.'

'That's what we do at The Camel's Ba – '

'Only,' interrupted Sam, 'I don't want anyone to know about it. Apart from you and me, that is.'

Jeremy's eyes searched Sam's face. Eventually he said, 'In my experience, that sort of thing generally implies an ulterior, and usually, ugly motive. People get annoyed.'

'You've done this sort of thing before then?'

'Now and again.'

'How much?'

'Depends on the job.'

'How much were you paid for your performance last week at the Pescatoria?'

Jeremy's smile vanished and he sat up. 'I thought I'd seen you before. You were the escort.' He got up suddenly. 'I don't think we've got any business to discuss.'

Sam put his hand on Jeremy's wrist and squeezed. Not enough to cause discomfort, but enough to imply that their discussion was not yet over. 'Don't panic,' he said. 'The deal is this. I'll double whatever you were paid.'

If there was any moral dilemma facing Jeremy's conscience, the battle was swiftly fought, and lucre won hands down. He dredged up one of his best, confident smiles and sat down again calmly. 'That's a very generous offer, if a little rash. I mean, I could think of a number, couldn't I?'

'You could,' said Sam, and reached into his pocket for

163

his chequebook and a pen. He could almost feel Jeremy's bright eyes boring into the back of his head as he signed and dated the cheque.

'I got two hundred pounds,' said Jeremy thickly.

Sam knew he was lying, but it didn't matter. He paused with the pen over the little black square with 'or order' written above it. 'Who employed you on Saturday night?' he asked simply. He heard Jeremy swallow loudly, saw his Adam's apple bob as his eyes flicked between the chequebook and Sam's face.

'I . . . I don't know,' he said eventually.

Sam looked up sharply, wary of Jeremy's wiles. But he saw that it was no act. He sighed and began putting his pen back into his jacket pocket.

'No wait,' said Jeremy urgently. 'It was all done by phone. The money came by postal order.' He looked away, seemingly angry with himself. 'I don't know why I let myself in for these things. I didn't like the sound of it much, but it was good money. And now you turn up the same day that I get another phone call from her.'

Fingers, cold and icy, played an arpeggio up and down Sam's spine.

'Her?' he said, his voice sounding odd. 'You said her?'

Jeremy nodded, studying Sam's face. 'She rang to say she wanted to meet me tonight. Said she was very pleased with my work and had another job for me. I couldn't meet her earlier, I'm rehearsing for something at the Sherman. Something modern. All black sets and polo-necks.'

'Her name?' breathed Sam, his eyes unfocused, staring into the distance.

'I don't know it. That's the truth. But I thought that if you were to come with me and stay out of sight, you could actually see her. Chances are you'll recognise her. I mean this sort of thing is usually set up by someone close to the victim.'

He was smiling as he watched Sam fill in the amount on the cheque.

* * *

164

They went in Sam's car and Jeremy directed them to a multi-storey NCP near the central station. Traffic was lightening, most people already having left for home. Sam parked in a grubby side-street behind a pub ostentatiously called The Philharmonic and they walked over to the car park.

'She said seven, on the roof. I'm supposed to stand near the lifts.' Jeremy laughed. 'All we need is a couple of zithers and for Orson Welles to walk round the corner, eh?'

Sam didn't smile. He was untouched by Jeremy's childlike enthusiasm and sense of adventure. Too many things had happened to him lately. Too many things that had wrenched his emotions. Someone, some unknown person, had been manipulating him. Messing with his life. And he didn't like it. He had to know, whoever it was.

Or whatever?

The thought struck him unawares. He'd suppressed the business of Jo's voice on the answerphone deliberately. Thinking about it was too painful. He still found it hard to believe that it was just possible it really was Jo. Jo trying to get a message to him. His rational mind rebelled at the evidence his own ears had presented.

Instead, he'd preferred to vent his frustration and anger in finding out who had been tangibly interfering in his affairs. But now the memory of that morning in Chloe's flat rose again. *Help me . . . help me . . .*

Stupid. It was stupid. This had nothing to do with Jo. It couldn't have. Jo couldn't send a bloody postal order to friend Jeremy from the other side.

But somebody did, Sammy.

Yes, somebody did.

Sam shivered and pulled his coat around him. It had become cold again. The drizzle of the afternoon had cleared but in its wake it had left an overcast, starless night. Inside the car park, petrol fumes hung like a sickly, cloying perfume in the damp and misty air. They walked up some narrow steps to the fourth floor and there parted company. Sam walked across the length of the floor towards a door marked Emergency Exit in the far corner. Jeremy was to continue up the stairs they'd shared thus far. The stairs that ran parallel to the lifts.

At the exit sign, Sam paused and signalled to Jeremy, who waved back cheerfully. His high spirits had manifested themselves in verbosity as they'd walked up the stairs. It was almost understandable. Jeremy was, after all, about to make £400.

Their stairwell Sam entered stank of stale urine and even staler disinfectant. He emerged on the roof into a silent, shadowy world. The mist damped down the noises from the street below and the visibility across the car park was lousy. Sam peered across and was relieved that he could make out Jeremy on the other side. He gave no sign of recognition; that had been the understanding. There were no more than twenty or so cars dotted about the roof. Sam saw Jeremy clapping his hands together for warmth as he paced back and forth in front of the squat, flat-roofed building that housed the lift winches. A car suddenly sputtered to life to his left and headlights pierced the mist. As was often the case in fog, the beams reflected off the water droplets that hung in the air and visibility suddenly became worse. Almost immediately, the driver dipped his lights and drove off slowly towards the down ramp.

Sam relaxed again and leaned against the cold concrete wall of his exit, hearing vague noises below as someone began to climb up.

And then lights came on from a car parked directly opposite where Jeremy had been standing. Sam stared hard but couldn't make out anything about its make or colour behind the twin beams. Jeremy stood, almost blinded, with both hands held out in front of him, trying to shield his eyes. He looked almost comical as Sam heard him ask, 'Hello? Is that you?'

The response from the driver of the car was instantaneous. The lights flicked down and up once and Jeremy began tentatively to walk towards them. There could not have been more than twenty yards between them.

Later, Sam would wonder just how fast a car might be travelling fifteen yards after accelerating from standing still.

Fast enough to send Jeremy hurtling backwards as the car scooped him off the concrete floor like a cowcatcher on an express train.

Fast enough for the noise of the collision to thud impossibly loudly in the dense night air.

Fast enough for the impact to twist Jeremy sideways in mid-air, flattening the top half of his body on to the bonnet like a broken rag doll.

The car accelerated towards the lift housing and Sam watched as friction began to drag Jeremy's body under the car. It looked almost as though the floor was swallowing him.

Jeremy's chest was parallel to the grille when the car began to brake with a porcine squeal. It was too late to prevent the car from hitting the building, but then, Sam supposed, the driver knew that well enough.

The contact between metal and concrete came with a sickening crunch, and inside that noise of screeching metal and tinkling glass, Sam knew that he heard a more woody, snapping noise. The noise of Jeremy's ribs cracking like so much kindling. There was also a scream, but it took a moment for Sam to realise that it was his own voice he was hearing.

For a few seconds after the impact, there was silence. A dense, breathless silence as Sam stared in horror at the tangled wreck of Jeremy's body pinioned against the wall.

It could only have been seconds before he heard excited, troubled voices from below him as people began to run up the stairway, attracted by the noise. But Sam could only watch, paralysed by nausea and horror, as the murderous car reversed sedately and began to wind its way down the ramp. It was such a cold-blooded, improbable sight that his mind hardly registered the facts he was later grateful for. He stared but didn't see until it was almost too late. But then a synapse fired and he saw that only one tail-light on the vehicle was working. And he logged the last three digits of the registration as LWO. But he knew it anyway. He recognised the car.

'The car was old, Sam. Old and ugly and white,' whispered Phipps's voice in his ear.

His breath heaved out of his chest as he swung back to look at Jeremy's crumpled, unmoving form on the floor of the car park. Even in the half-light, he could see that Jeremy's shape had doubled as a slowly expanding shadow engulfed him. Dimly, Sam realised that the shadow was a pool of Jeremy's blood.

A scream brought him to his senses. Someone ran out of the lift exit and almost fell over what was left of Jeremy, uttering a screech as he or she did so. At the same time, people emerged from the stairs behind Sam and rushed past him shouting questions.

Sam saw them go with a cold detachment, as if he were watching from some point outside his body. His mind held two images. One was of what was happening in front of him – people shouting and yelling for help. The other was an imagined scene, vivid in its horror, which showed the car that had killed Jeremy. Remorseless, it drifted slowly down the ramps as people ignored it and ran up to the roof to see what all the bother was.

'The car was old, Sam. Old and ugly and white.'

Ignored it as it drifted right by them.

Hate is waiting for you, Sam.

A car driven by a killer who had set Jeremy up.

Set him up and killed him with a tried-and-tested method.

Tried and tested on . . .

Hate is waiting . . .

Sam turned and ran.

Chapter Twelve

He flew down the stairs recklessly, four, sometimes five at a time. He bumped past people who stared after him as if he were a madman. It was a miracle that he didn't fall and break his neck.

What about Jeremy? I should have stayed to help. Should have at least tried.

But in his heart he knew there was nothing he could have done. Others could call an ambulance as well as he could. But even as he thought it, the memory of the sickening crunch Jeremy's ribcage had made told him that it was a waste of time.

He burst out of the exit and sprinted to his car. He roared to the end of the block, took a right and screeched to a halt on a zebra crossing, suffering evil glances from a man with a ruck-sack.

'You ought to look where you're go – '

He roared on, not waiting to hear the end of the tirade. He took another right and saw LWO pulling out into traffic queuing at some lights twenty yards ahead. He stopped at a junction. The solid line of cars in front of him did not look disposed to let him in. Sam pulled out as the lights changed, heedless of the horns of irate drivers and prayed that the lights would hold until he got through.

He made it on orange.

He stayed behind the car for twenty minutes as it wound its way towards the docks. He hovered two, sometimes three cars behind. Far enough to avoid detection, he hoped. But also too far to get any real view of the driver. It was, in any case, hopeless from the back as the head was hooded. The car was an old white Marina, exhaust hanging precariously low. A real rust bucket.

A murderous rust bucket.

Once, he felt like ramming it, the urge to destroy it almost overwhelming. But the moment had passed as the Marina made for the docks.

After Bute Street, he lost his bearings in a series of smaller and smaller side-streets. He regained them again as he drove past the Royal Hamadryad Hospital, but had only the vaguest idea of his actual whereabouts when the car took a left at a junction which had a red-topped T sign over it. He decided it would be foolish to follow the Marina up a dead end and instead drove on for twenty yards and parked. He could hear the noise of water and knew that he must be very near to the river.

The lights of Penarth twinkled across the flats and as he walked back, he heard the scrape of metal on concrete and the shuddering protesting of a badly hung door. He turned the final corner to find himself in a poorly lit lane. On either side was a series of garages, sixteen in all. They were old, with zinc-sheeted roofs and black-painted double wooden doors. Halfway down, one set of doors was open and a red light glowed from beneath. As he watched, he saw the red light dim and in its place a brighter, yellow light come on. The doors began to swing shut.

He was toying with the idea of getting closer, of challenging whoever was inside, when he saw something that stopped him dead.

A foot came forward to push away a half-brick that had been placed to stop the door from swinging shut when the car was driven in. Its owner remained hidden by the nearest of the double doors, but above the foot a leg emerged visible to the knee. It was booted to mid-calf, but above the boot Sam saw flesh clad in dark nylon.

A woman's legs.

Above, a head, distorted grotesquely by shadow, danced in silhouette through the grimy windows of the doors.

Instinctively, Sam ducked into the shadows in case she emerged, his breath catching in his throat, but all he heard were the doors shutting and a bolt being pulled across. He readied himself for the confrontation. The lane was a dead end after all. She would have to walk out past him.

She'll be out in a minute, Sam. You can spit in her stinking face in just a minute.

But the minute turned into three, and then into five and still there was no sign. After his forced inactivity, he was feeling the cold begin to bite into him. He moved out of his hiding-place and saw with some consternation that there was no longer any light on in the garage. It was the fourth one along in the row. Now it looked as deserted as if no one had been near it for days.

Puzzled, he walked along to the locked doors and listened. All was silent; no one was about. There was a grimy window set high up in each of the doors. But it was no good, there was nothing at all to see except the pitch-darkness. With a growing sense of disquiet, he retraced his steps to the end of the lane.

Why would anyone want to sit in an unlit garage for ten minutes?

Reassuring himself that his car was still parked and safe, he turned and walked back along the poorly lit street, past the gable end of a derelict end-of-terrace house, its dark, glassless windows staring down at him disapprovingly. Beyond it, guarded by a rusting iron swing gate, was a narrow pathway. The gate opened with surprising quiet as Sam took a few faltering steps down the dark footpath.

A chain-link fence separated it on one side from a jumble of untidy gardens backing on to dilapidated houses. But it was the wall on the other side that held

Sam's attention. The wall that his instinct had told him must be there. He walked slowly along the path, staring at the brick wall, halting at the first door he saw set into the brick. He walked on and counted three more. Opposite the fourth he stopped and in the dim illumination shed by the kitchen lights of the houses behind, he saw that in this door the Yale lock was new and sturdy. It resisted his half-hearted shove easily.

She hadn't sat in the darkened garage for ten minutes at all. She had locked up and left almost immediately through this other door, conveniently placed for the use of the home owners who lived on the other side of the chain-link fence. Left while Sam had hidden like a nervous schoolboy in the shadows.

Idiot! You bloody idiot!

Somewhere in the dank distance, Sam heard a clock begin to strike the hour, his mind counting out the chimes unbidden as he tried to set the dreadful, terrifying thoughts that tortured his mind into some sort of order.

Clang . . .

He heard Ned Whelan's carping voice say: '*There was something odd about her, wasn't there?*'

. . . Clang . . .

'*She was waiting for you, Sam.*'

. . . Clang . . .

Waiting when you found your car stuck up with glue.
'*Only a hair's breadth away from being sectioned.*'

. . . Clang . . .

She could have glued the car herself . . . It virtually forced you into accepting her lift, didn't it?

No, said a voice inside him.

. . . Clang . . .

And didn't the magazines just happen to appear after she'd been in the flat?

No, please . . .

. . . Clang . . .

She could have set herself up with Jeremy. Set herself

172

up to look like the victim. *And you're a real sucker for victims, aren't you, Sammy? You didn't need a second invitation after that, eh?*

. . . Clang . . .

The memory of Chloe's bed suddenly filled Sam with revulsion. That he could have touched the monster who had killed Jo was beyond contemplation, that he could have made . . . love – '

A wail, the vocal distillation of his own stupid gullibility and anguish, escaped Sam's lips like a murky bubble rising from the depths of some dark, bottomless lake. Something Paul had said floated close to the surface of memory, but he couldn't remember it. Something that Debbie had told him. Something about Jo and Chloe . . . A hitch? Something about a hitch.

Oh dear God, no. What if Jo had had second thoughts? What if she had seen something or found out something about Chloe that had made her want to break off the relationship? Something about her mental state, perhaps? What if Chloe hadn't liked it? What if she had thought of some sick sociopathic revenge? An ultimate revenge?

He felt hot bile in his throat as the monstrous thoughts filled his mind.

What if she had killed Jo and then lain in wait for him to return? Lain in wait and then slowly, poisonously begun to inveigle her way into his life? Making him sympathise with her, making him sleep with her, making him give her all the things that Jo had promised her and more. The enormity of it staggered him. Phipps, the car, the answerphone message. All designed to break down his resistance with the added appeal of twisting a knife in the wound.

A slime worm. A vicious, patient slime worm that curled up to its unsuspecting victim and paralysed it before slowly sucking out all the living juices while its meal writhed in agony.

And he had told her of Debbie's misgivings. Told her

173

that Debbie had suspected something had been wrong with the partnership.

Fear clutched at his heart like the fingers of a drowning man.

Debbie.

He thought suddenly of Debbie.

Debbie, who believed she knew what Jo had been trying to tell her. Debbie, at whose house he was meant to meet Chloe Jesson that very evening.

His brain registered the chimes and he tore back his sleeve and stared at his watch. He'd been wandering around for almost fifteen minutes. It was eight already. They were meant to have been at Debbie's at seven-thirty.

His fear crystallised into an instant stab of realisation. It was nearly twenty minutes since she'd entered and left the garage. *She* could already be there.

He thought of Paul's overtime and Debbie being alone in the house. Debbie alone with *her*.

He didn't stop to think any more. There was no time to waste with the garage.

He just ran as fast as his trembling legs could carry him.

Chapter Thirteen

Sam had never been an overtly religious man. He considered his values and attitudes humanitarian rather than purely 'Christian', although he felt that essentially they were one and the same. He wasn't particularly fond of the Church. He considered it austere, anachronistic and responsible for as much harm as purported good. His experience with people zealous enough to worship regularly and demonstratively had done nothing to alter his opinion. Hypocrisy was the word that most often sprang to mind whenever he thought of those supposedly lucky enough to have been born again. But as he pulled up in that quiet cul-de-sac, his mind voiced a prayer for help and guidance from a source that was beyond understanding.

Please God, let me be in time. Please God.

The sight of Paul's brassy black Capri with its lights on outside the house almost made him cry out in relief.

He screeched to a halt and ran up the path. There were lights on in several rooms. He rang the bell, keeping his finger pressed firmly down, and simultaneously pounded on the brass knocker, rusty from lack of use. He kept his face pressed against the frosted-glass panel, anxious for any sign of movement from within. At last, after what seemed like an age, he saw a blur of movement as someone approached.

It was Paul who answered. Sam could hear the irritation in his voice as he berated the impatient caller from inside the hall.

'Jesus H. Christ, all right, all right. Where's the bloody fire? Sam?'

Paul's tirade shut off abruptly as Sam bustled in before the door was fully open. He reached forward and grabbed Paul's arm in a vice-like grip.

'Where's Debbie?'

Paul's face registered bemused consternation. 'Upstairs.'

'You're sure?' The urgency in Sam's tone cut through the air between them.

'Yes, but I've only just got in myself. I haven't even seen Deb yet. I just yelled hello and she answered from up there. She's probably changing. I – '

'Check,' barked Sam and there was something in his voice that dissipated any argument Paul had thought of putting up. He turned and shouted up the stairwell.

'Deb? You OK?'

The reply came back muffled but unmistakable. 'Yes. Why?'

Sam's eyes squeezed shut in relief.

'Uh, Sam's here,' said Paul inspirationally.

At the top of the stairs, Debbie appeared, a tight black dress clinging to her body with easy elegance, her hands busy at an earlobe with something large and glittering. Leaning over the banister, she beamed down at Sam.

'Hi, Sam. Won't be a minute. Paul, get Sam a drink.'

She turned to re-enter the bedroom. It was Paul who stopped her, his voice loaded with apology.

'Deb, luv, I have to go out again.'

'Oh Paul,' she wailed without turning back to face them.

'Some maniac has mashed someone against a wall in the multi-storey near the station. The call came in just as I was pulling up. They need some extra hands to take statements down there. I'll be as quick as I can.'

Debbie turned on a three-inch heel, her face resigned, eyelids suddenly heavy. 'Well at least wait until I get down.' She turned again. This time the door shut after

176

her, leaving Sam with his cheeks burning and Paul with a hangdog expression.

'I'm really sorry, Sam. We've got two off sick – '

'I saw it.' His words were low and urgent, slicing across Paul's apology like an axe.

Paul blinked. 'Saw what?'

'The car park. I was there . . .'

The blinking turned into a stare of dumbstruck horror. This time it was Paul's turn to take Sam's arm. With a glance up the stairs, he pulled Sam into the kitchen and closed the door. When he spoke next it was in an urgent whisper.

'I'm all ears, Sam.'

'I saw it,' repeated Sam. 'I was with the victim until a minute before it happened. An actor. And it was no accident. She set it up. She knew I was going to see him, knew I was going to find out . . . Jesus, Paul, she mowed him down.' Sam ran his hands through his hair. Paul saw that they were shaking badly.

'Who, Sam, who?'

'Chloe. It was the actor she killed. The actor who threatened her in the restaurant. She knew I was going looking . . . She must have set herself up . . .'

'Christ,' said Paul, and then saw that Sam's shake had spread to his legs. 'Sam, you want something?'

Sam shook his head and continued. 'I followed the car to a lock-up garage in the docks. Caldicott Lane. Fourth one in. The car is inside . . . The car she used to kill Jo.'

'Sam, what the fuck are you talking about?'

'Don't you understand?' implored Sam. 'She did it all, set it all up. She's been waiting months for me to get back.'

'Why, Sam?'

Sam held Paul's gaze in silence. Finally he said, 'Do you believe in evil, Paul?'

Paul's face tightened into a grim mask. 'Where is she now?'

Sam waved a hand at the dark night outside the window. 'Out there, somewhere.'

Paul heaved a sigh. 'Stay here with Debbie. I'll go to the lock-up, get an APB out on Chloe, uhh, Jesson, right?'

Sam nodded defeatedly. Paul took both his elbows in his hands and forced Sam to look into his face. 'Did you hear me, Sam? Stay here with Debbie.'

Then he turned and left.

Sam was crossing the hall when Debbie called to him from the top of the stairs.

'Sam,' she said, smiling. 'I thought I heard the door slam?'

'Paul had to leave.'

Something in his voice made her hesitate. She came down the stairs towards him. 'Sam, what's wrong?'

'Another murder.'

'Oh God.'

Sam shuddered. 'I watched a man being crushed to death this afternoon. The man she employed to trick me into sympathising with her.'

'Chloe?' said Debbie, aghast.

Sam nodded painfully. 'I couldn't see it, couldn't see right in front of my face – '

'Shhh,' said Debbie, stroking his face gently. 'It's all right. It's all right.'

They stood that way for a while, Sam almost overcome with relief, glad of the warmth and comfort of her proximity. Eventually, Debbie led him into the living room and sat him down with a drink. He felt a little better afterwards.

'Will it help to talk?' she asked.

Sam looked at her and smiled gratefully.

Paul was met at the address Sam had given him by two uniformed constables. One stayed in the front whilst the other went with Paul along the narrow path to the back entrance, where Paul set to work with a tyre lever. The door had a Yale lock, but the wood was old and gave after not much effort. The noise of splintering timber brought no curious faces or nosy neighbours. The only response was the barking of a dog somewhere. Paul knew that the area was one where the noise of a door yielding to a prising tyre lever was no novelty.

He pushed the door open and shone his light inside. It was a small space, most of it taken up by the big white car. There was hardly enough room to stroke a cat, let along swing one. His beam found a switch on the wall and he flicked it on. A single naked light-bulb glowed into life and illuminated the dusty, dingy garage. But Paul hardly noticed the cobwebs and the filth. His attention was riveted by the car. It sat, squat and ugly, like some sleeping animal.

'What's this all about, Paul?' asked the uniformed man, but Paul didn't reply. His gaze was transfixed by what was left of the front of the car.

It was a crumpled, twisted mess. The bumper hung off and on one side the headlight was completely missing, its socket staring up at him at an unnatural angle. The grille was battered and Paul saw some material hanging there, the remains of some garment. There was blood, too, and small fragments of bone mingled with what could well have been lung tissue.

Paul swallowed back the hot acid that was rising in his throat and looked over the rest of the bonnet. The whole of it was damaged, but further towards the centre the paintwork looked particularly battered. The damage there had all the hallmarks of age. Where the metal had buckled and bent, thin lines of rust had appeared. His eyes followed the curve of the metal down to the grille, where a huge dent was obvious. There, his sickened disbelieving eyes saw some more material, different from the cleaner, newer khaki that had struck him initially. This was a fine black-and-white check, a dogtooth pattern that was dark and dirty, but recognisable nonetheless.

179

Jo had been wearing trousers made of the same material the night she died.

Suddenly, he could no longer hold back the rising tide of his nausea. He had been to the scene of many murders, had remained detached and pragmatic, but he was diving into new depths here. This was a murder weapon that had killed three at least. The actor, Phipps and Jo.

And Jo.

Knowing the victims made a huge difference, he realised, but there was something else to this.

A murderous witch had targeted his sister-in-law. Someone he had cared for. Why? What possible reason could she have had for doing such a thing to someone who had helped her? Who wanted to go into business with her?

He turned away from the car and was shudderingly, violently sick. He let it all come, sweating and feeling hot despite the coldness of the air. When he finished he felt wretched, leaning against the rough brickwork, his whole body trembling uncontrollably.

The uniformed man asked, 'Hey, is this something to do with that smash-up in the multi-storey?'

'And more,' said Paul grimly. He couldn't look at the car any more. He couldn't bear to. As his raw eyes stared about him he saw a small bench against a wall just to the side of the door through which he'd forced his entry. Initially, what he saw was a jumble of papers, but as he peered, he realised that they were photographs. He took a couple of steps towards the bench and stared in total disbelief. There were several snapshots pinned roughly to a wooden board. They hung at odd angles from red-topped drawing-pins and to his amazement he saw that they were mainly of Sam. Mostly candid shots and close-ups.

And then his eyes saw that there were others, of a girl, a pretty auburn-haired girl full of smiling joy and life.

Jo.

His mind reeled.

For what seemed like hours, his eyes remained glued to the photographs, his mind grasping for some sort of explanation.

'Shit, look at all this stuff,' said the policeman. 'Talk about weird.'

Paul looked across at the far wall where the uniformed man was leaning over a small shelf at thigh level.

Dolls.

It was covered in dolls. Life-like, baby pink, in various stages of undress. Or rather, he thought when he looked more closely, in various stages of dress. Only they weren't dolls' clothes. They were expensive children's clothes. Some with the price tags still dangling from smooth necks. And in the middle, pinned by a tack at each corner, was one more photograph. A bigger one, ten by eight. A girl, the same auburn hair, the same even-toothed smile as the pictures on the wall. But as he studied it, he saw that there were subtle differences. Invisible to the casual observer, invisible to many who knew them. But not to Paul. Debbie had been his wife for ten years. It wasn't Jo he was looking at. This last photograph was of Debbie.

He swung away from the bench, his eyes wild and staring. The car stared back at him malevolently, its chromework distorted in a lunatic, lopsided grin.

This was a room of death. He could smell it, taste it, feel it in his bones.

This was a temple. She kept the car here. Had kept it locked away here ever since Jo . . .

There was evil in this room, he could feel it radiating from the car, feel it pressing down on him.

He turned back to the photographs and the dolls.

It's a shrine. Dear God, it's a shrine for all her victims.

'But why?' he cried. 'Why, in God's name, why?'

The uniformed man was squatting on the floor, shining his torch on something he'd found there. 'Hey Paul, you'd better take a look at this.'

He picked up a large ten-by-eight black-and-white

glossy and handed it to Paul. The photograph had been mutilated, scratched and raked by some sharp instrument, burned with cigarette butts. A moan escaped Paul's lips. A moan of despair and desperation. He threw the photograph down on the bench and rushed past his colleague without uttering a word.

'Where the hell are you going?' came the question shouted after him.

But Paul didn't hear. He was already on his way to his car.

Already on his way back to the house. Driven by the knowledge of who had murdered Jo and Jeremy.

In the darkness of the garage, the uniformed man looked up to see his colleague standing in the doorway.

'What's up with him?'

'Took one look at this and left like a bat out of hell.' He handed the mutilated photograph to his partner, who fingered it and began tracing the burn marks on its surface. His fingers traced a name.

Chloe.

Debbie stood and refilled Sam's glass. She had listened impassively yet sympathetically to Sam's outpourings, her eyes sharing his pain.

As she returned with his drink, Sam noticed the preoccupation in her face as if for the first time.

'Debbie, I'm sorry if I've frightened you.'

Debbie smiled. 'As long as you're here, I'm not frightened.'

'Good,' said Sam. He ran his fingers through his hair. 'I can't believe how stupid I've been. I should have listened to you, Debbie. I didn't want to believe that Jo had told you about Chloe, I see that now.'

He saw her face cloud slightly. 'But knowing about Chloe doesn't change anything, does it?'

'What do you mean?'

'It doesn't change the fact that Jo has been trying to tell us something?'

'Debbie,' said Sam patiently. 'I don't understand all of this. I don't pretend to, but it's over now. They'll find her. They'll – '

Debbie put her fingers to his lips. 'Shhh,' she quietened him. 'It doesn't change what Jo has been trying to tell me.'

'Debbie . . .'

'Please, Sam. I was going to tell you tonight anyway. Tell you especially. It's ironic we're both here together. Just the two of us.'

Sam frowned. Debbie's face glowed with expectation. He felt helpless in the light of that glow. He wanted to stop her, tell her to shut up, but the answerphone message haunted him. He knew now that it had been merely a cruel joke on Chloe's part. Another sadistic prank to please her twisted mind. And yet he heard it in his mind over and over, such a plaintive cry. *Help me . . . help me . . .*

'It should have been me who got pregnant, not Jo. You do realise that, don't you?' Her tone was light, casual, deceptive.

Sam nodded, relieved. 'Jo was very anxious about telling you. The last thing either of us wanted was to hurt your feelings, after what you'd been through. So Mary told Maude, right?'

Debbie held his gaze, her face rapt. 'That's what Jo has been trying to tell me, Sam. She's been trying to make amends.'

'Amends?'

'She wants me to have her baby, Sam.'

'What?' Sam's question came after several seconds of incredulous silence.

Debbie repeated calmly, 'Jo wants me to have her baby.'

Sam put down his drink, this final revelation almost too much to bear. To his consternation, he felt a tear moisten his eye. A tear of hopelessness and longing, of grief for his unborn child and dead wife. Debbie's arcane words had triggered off an emotional response for which he was unprepared. He bit back the words that threatened to leap out of his mouth. Words of condemnation and ridicule.

'You must listen, Sam,' urged Debbie. 'It's so obvious. I should have realised long ago . . .' She had her fingers on his shirt, undoing the top button.

Sam trembled. The horror of the day was setting in. He felt powerless. An inanimate object watching Debbie's deft fingers open the buttons. 'Debbie, what are you doing?'

She smiled at him, her lips parting slightly. Her hands were on his skin, running over his shoulders. She stood and pulled his hands to her thighs, guiding his fingers under her skirt until they met with the naked flesh above her stocking tops. Sam was shaking his head, his lips trembling in a dilemma of desire and guilt. It was wrong, all wrong, but he was overwhelmed by the onslaught to his senses.

'This is what Jo wants, Sam,' said Debbie, squirming ecstatically in his hands. She leaned forward and kissed him, her tongue darting and hungry.

Sam moaned beneath her as she pushed him down on to the settee. It was a strangled moan, the words contained within it coming out tinny and hollow.

'Paul . . . What about Paul?'

She was above him, her dress already over her head. The lighting was dim. And as he stared at her, she lifted her head and laughed at the ridiculousness of his question. It was a parody of Jo's carefree laugh, laced with husky desire. Her skin shone like Jo's. Her eyes glinted like Jo's.

Sam was helpless under the onslaught as she stripped him, rousing him with her mouth and tongue, sliding him into her with moist deliciousness.

'I've waited so long, Sam,' she breathed. 'Waited so lo – '

The noise came unexpectedly.

'Listen,' commanded Sam, cutting her off.

And it came again. Muffled but unmistakable. A dull clunk.

Sam scrambled up from beneath her. 'It's her,' he said.

'No. It's just the door banging in the wind,' said Debbie, reaching for him.

'There is no wind,' he said and got up. He went to the door, pulling on his shirt and trousers, his head at an angle, alert and listening.

'Please come back,' said Debbie urgently. 'I need you, Sam.'

'She's outside.' He shuddered.

'Sam,' wailed Debbie. 'Please. Don't leave me.'

Clunk, went the noise again.

In the kitchen, he saw nothing but the scattered signs of food preparation. It looked ordered and neat. A door led off into a utility room. He remembered that from there a door opened into the garage.

Clunk. Louder this time.

He walked across to the utility room and switched on the light. He peered through a glass pane in the door. There was nothing there. A washing-machine, a tumble-drier, nothing that could make a noise like . . .

Clunk.

The garage. It was coming from the garage.

He walked through the utility room and opened the connecting door. Black night engulfed him in a freezing embrace that took his breath away. The concrete floor felt cold and sharp against his bare feet as the damp air seeped into them. He reached for the light switch and got nothing in response. There was a car in the garage. In the dim light it was difficult to make out a colour.

Cursing, Sam stumbled through the wedge of illumination that sprang out from the open utility-room door and stood to one side, allowing the light to get in past him, to show him what he wanted to see. Recognition dawned on him.

185

He had driven this car. Chloe's car.

Clunk . . .

The noise was much louder now, from the far side of the car. What the hell was it doing here?

He moved carefully around to the flank and found himself in the dense, blinding darkness of the vehicle's shadow. By touch more than vision, he felt his way around the front end, his senses straining. When yet another *CLUNK* came, he was within nearly three feet of the source and it almost made him lose his skin.

Then he knew what it was. The sound of a car door opening and banging against something else, something wooden. Cautiously, his eyes gradually adjusting but still unable to penetrate the deep shadow on the far side of the car, he moved around. He saw that it was the rear, passenger side-door that was open. Crouching, he crept forward, close enough to put his hand on the edge of the door, close enough to put his head gingerly over the top to see what was inside.

What he saw set his mind reeling.

It was Chloe, terrified eyes wide and staring, her mouth taped over, her hands and legs roughly tied with thin flex. She was slumped across the back seat. It was her legs, bent at right angles, that were pushing the door out so that it banged against a wooden upright in the garage. Somehow she must have opened it and had been trying to signal.

She had manoeuvred herself so that she lay along the back seat, her knees bent and thrusting. She immediately began to make whimpering noises through the gag, and it was difficult to know whether she was coughing or not, but her eyes were full of terrified relief. Despite her obvious urgings, Sam, for a moment, could only stare in total dumb amazement and disbelief at what was before him. It wasn't so much the numbing horror of it all, it was more the way his mind shied away from the meaning of what he was seeing.

Her moaning became more urgent as his inability to

move became protracted. In desperation, she thrust the door again.

Clunk.

The noise broke Sam's spell.

He clambered in, reaching for the bonds and the gag. She spluttered and gasped, her words high-pitched and hysterical:

'I thought no one would come. I thought no one would come.' She grabbed for Sam convulsively as he sat her up.

Sam felt numb, his hands clay-like, unable to respond, unwilling to comfort the woman who just moments before had been the object of his hate and fear.

She was sobbing in his arms as he patted her back ineffectually, the staggering enormity of finding her tied and bleeding threatening to push his teetering brain over the brink of reason. This couldn't be happening. What about the garage? What about those stockinged legs? What about –

'Whu . . . whu . . . where is sh . . . she?' Chloe was trying to speak, her eyes terrified white orbs.

'Who?' asked Sam. 'Who did this to you?'

Chloe screamed.

She screamed because the light that was streaming in from the utility-room was suddenly extinguished with the slamming of a door.

Instantly, they were plunged into a sepulchral darkness. For a long moment there was absolute silence as breath locked in throats and hearts almost stopped. And then Chloe began to sob urgently again.

'Close the doors!' she screamed. 'Lock the doors, Sam. Please lock the doors.'

She was scrambling over him, trying to pull the door to and all he could do was get in her way.

'Lock them, please.' Her voice rasped and rose and fell in total desperation. At first Sam simply sat there in bewilderment, but her remonstrations were so overwhelming that he did reach forward and press his hand down on the catches that locked the front doors.

187

Finally, when she was happy that they were secure, Chloe began to sink down, crouching low in the well between front and back seats, whimpering quietly.

'Chloe,' said Sam, 'we have to get out of here.'

He felt rather than saw her shake her head. It brushed against his knee. He reached down and spoke gently as if to a child.

'Why? Why can't we?'

'Can't you feel it?' breathed Chloe. She reached up and grasped his hand. He felt it shaking uncontrollably.

'Feel what?' he asked in bewilderment.

'Feel *her*.'

'Who?'

From outside, in the darkness of the garage, Sam heard the voice that froze his heart.

'Maudie wants her baby, Sam.'

It was a small, plaintive, childlike voice and it sent Sam reeling. His fragile sanity, teetering already, now slipped over the thin edge. In the Stygian darkness he whispered:

'Jo . . .'

Beneath him, Chloe was crying softly, but hearing him voice the name she said, 'No, Sam. No.'

But Sam was beyond reason. He could only sit and let his untethered mind wander.

He hardly even noticed the thin scraping noise, high-pitched and nerve-jangling, that began at the rear windscreen and traced a screeching line around the car.

But Chloe could hear it. Her eyes darted up and back, searching for the source, seeing nothing except the faintest outline of a dark shape moving outside the windows and the half-seen tip of a long, thin blade being dragged against the windows. She rammed her fist into her mouth to prevent the scream of terror that rose there from escaping.

'Maudie wants her baby, Sam,' said the voice again and Sam shuddered.

Mercifully, it signalled the end of the dreadful

scraping. For long seconds there was nothing except the loud beating of two racing hearts inside the car.

Whump.

The noise, impossibly loud, was followed by the tinkling of glass shards as the windscreen shattered under the impact of some heavy tool.

Chloe screamed. So did Sam.

They waited for the second blow, but it never came.

Light!

There was light.

The utility-room door swung open and a voice said: 'Sam? Debbie?'

Silhouetted in the doorway was Paul. Large, worried Paul. He took two steps into the dark garage before something hard and metallic cleaved away his right eyebrow, missing his eye by millimetres. He staggered back, holding up his arms flailingly as blows, rapid and incredibly forceful, rained down upon him. Many found their mark, on his face, chest, upper arms. Screaming, he turned and stumbled backwards, overwhelmed by the ferocity of the attack.

The knife followed him.

Chloe, watching from the car but seeing only the blur of shapes, yelled:

'Get out, get out!'

Once again she reached over Sam, this time pushing the door open. In moments she was outside, running for the garage door, reaching down for the handle and turning it, slipping once, yanking at it on her knees.

All the while, Sam sat in the car and watched her.

Finally, with a muted roar, the garage door swung up. With one eye on the utility-room door, she ran back to the car and began pulling Sam out. He felt leaden, a flesh doll. He came reluctantly, his eyes unfocused.

Chloe was screaming at him.

'Come on, for God's sake. We must run. Sam, what is the matter with you?'

She was jerking at his arm, pulling him towards the

door. Finally, he focused on her face and what she saw there was heart-rending. He shook his head.

'No. I can't.'

'Please,' she begged, crying now. 'Please, Sam, please.'

His eyes glazed over again and a distant smile wafted over his lips. 'I'm sorry I doubted you . . .'

Chloe stared at him, bewildered. 'Doubted me?'

But his eyes had drifted back to the inner world that she couldn't penetrate. 'Jo . . .' he mumbled. 'I have to go back.'

'No, Sam. No – '

But already he was turning away from her.

She stared at him through tears of impotence, her arms waving aimlessly in the air after him.

And then she was running, sobbing, terrified. She saw Paul's car, the engine still running, the door still open, slewed across the drive.

She burned five ounces of rubber as she took off, her eyes glued to the road ahead, never daring to stray to the rear-view mirror for fear of what she might see following her.

Chapter Fourteen

She drove two hundred yards before the car screeched to a halt in the middle of the road.

Outside, a drizzle spattered against the windshield as the wipers beat metronomically, chiding her with a repetitive taunt.

Running away.

Running away.

Running away.

Inside, her head slumped against the wheel, Chloe fought with the thin, demanding inner voice that had made her stop. It told her that she couldn't do it. Couldn't leave him to God alone knew what fate back in that house.

But a part of her said, Yes, yes, of course she could. They were all insane. It was no business of hers. Christ, she had only met the guy a few days ago. Really met him. He meant nothing to her. A fling, that's all it had been.

Then why wasn't she speeding away like a bat out of hell? She should get to a phone box and ring for help. That was the logical thing. There was no other option, was there?

Groaning, Chloe lifted her head off the wheel and, craning her neck, took a swift peek at herself in the rear-view. The face that looked back at her was straight out of the *Twilight Zone*. Zombie mascara rings rimmed her eyes. Blood from a wound on her temple had become crusted and dark, matting her hair into a black lump. The dirt-caked cheeks were traversed by clear tramlines left by her tears. She wiped away a glob of mucus from her nostril in disgust.

'Shit,' she said. And the sheer absurdity of the streak of vanity that prompted her shocked response did two things simultaneously. It repulsed her and, at the same time, a smile of ridicule touched her lips.

Just who did she think she was kidding.

Running away was not really her style. She'd done it once and it had left a bad, sour taste in her mouth. She'd let herself be manipulated and lied to herself that it had been the best – the only – option. But all it had been was an unhappy lie.

She felt cold, bottomless fear grip her as she thought of what she was contemplating, but at the same time it felt right. And that feeling was a rare and delicious one, like the discovery of a beautiful flower amidst a bed of choking weeds.

Cursing to herself, she swung the car around in a tight circle and headed back to the house.

The street was deserted as she cruised up to the pavement. She stopped, the engine still running, and stared across. The front door hung open, spilling light on to the small patch of lawn at the front.

The house was still. It seemed to her like some large animal, sitting and waiting.

Wiping away the dirt from her face, Chloe steeled herself.

'You're an idiot, Jesson,' she murmured as she stepped out into the damp air.

Stealthily, she crept up towards the front door, not daring to call his name.

It was wide open, the hall empty. She stepped inside, her heart hammering in her chest, threatening to leap-frog into her mouth at any moment. In one corner, next to a wooden settle, she saw a dark bundle on the floor. She peered at it, her legs threatening to fold beneath her like deck-chairs as she saw it was the body of a man. Around his unmoving head, a dark port-wine halo stained the beige carpet, glistening thickly. Above, on the wall, smudges of red culminating in a sweeping, descending arc told a graphic tale of violence. She took one more step and stopped.

The bundle moved. A hand strayed semi-consciously upwards towards the damaged head and then flopped back.

Covering the shoulders was a yellow-striped shirt.

Sam had been wearing blue.

She turned quickly, shifting her attention to the other door leading off the hall. It stood slightly ajar, a soft amber light glowing within. And there were voices.

Slowly, she took a step towards it, pausing outside to listen, peeking through the crack between door and jamb, frustrated at not being able to see.

Gently, she pushed the door open.

No creaks, just smooth, oiled motion.

Thank the Lord for 3-in-1, she thought.

The scene that greeted her as the door swung open set her flesh crawling.

Sam was kneeling, his shirt pulled down around his waist, his face vacuous as he listened to the woman talk to him. Listened and let the poison seep into his head. And as Chloe looked she knew that Sam was losing it. It didn't matter what was going to happen here, if she didn't get him back from whatever place his mind was on a one-way trip to, it wouldn't matter.

She watched in sick fascination as Debbie danced around him in a slow waltz, clutching in her arms and to her face a doll. She saw the hand press the doll's soft stomach and heard the thing cry . . .

Will you be my mummy?

Debbie still held the knife. Except that it wasn't silver any more. It looked as if someone had used it as a dipstick. But it wasn't oil that was coating the end.

Will you . . .

Debbie ran the knife down Sam's back. She was humming to herself, clutching the doll in her other hand.

. . . be my . . .

Sam arched his back and a grimace of pain stretched his face.

. . . mummy?

Where it had left his flesh there was blood running. And then she was in front of him, apologising.

'I have to do it. I have to punish you. You killed Mary, oh yes you did.'

She fell to her knees in front of him, her hands holding his face, kissing him, caressing his eyes, her hands around his neck, the knife sticking up like a flag-pole. And Chloe saw Sam's hand come up slowly and caress the wrist that held the knife. She saw him tug the wrist gently and hope flared brightly in her mind. She watched as Sam manoeuvred it so that the knife lay against his throat.

No, Sam, not that! a voice screamed in her head.

She didn't want to throw up, although she felt like it then. She knew she was witnessing an obscene travesty. A scene from someone else's nightmare. Sam's nightmare.

In front of her, Debbie pulled back her face suddenly animated with fury.

'Kiss me, you bastard. Kiss me. Don't you know who I am? Kiss Jo, baby. Kiss Jo. Jo wants you to fuck me, Sam. She took my baby. I want you to give me it back.'

Sam was trembling, his arms quivering at his sides. Chloe could see that some inner battle raged within him. An ancient battle. He forced himself to look at the face of the woman in front of him, her eyes wild, feral. And in the silence, Chloe heard the doll's innards winding down to a stop before Sam whispered in a voice laden with grief and confusion:

'Jo . . .'

Understanding filled Chloe with a hot lava of anger. He had been lying to himself all this time. Superficially, he had dismissed all that had happened, but Chloe saw that within, deep inside the well of his being, he had

194

wanted to believe. He wanted Jo to be here in this house desperately, achingly. The image of his hand on the knife played back in her mind and she knew that if he did not find Jo physically, then he meant to join her soul. She felt for him with a bolt of emotion so strong it shook her. And she knew this was more than any man should endure. A horrifying, cruel trick.

'Sam,' she said softly. 'Sam.'

The sound of her voice made Sam and Debbie's necks swivel round in Chloe's direction. Debbie's eyes seemed to burn and flicker like an ember caught in a draught as Chloe said:

'It isn't Jo, Sam. It isn't.'

'Shut up you slut,' screamed Debbie.

And then Chloe was in the room, holding her hand out to him, reaching for him.

Sam was shaking his head in denial. It all made perfect sense to him, couldn't she see? The magazines, the perfume. It was Jo. It had to be Jo.

'She did it all, can't you see that,' pleaded Chloe. 'She's sick, Sam. She's – '

Debbie flew at her like some crazed animal, clawing, flailing with the knife. And Sam watched it all like a man in a sick dream. Chloe fell back under the assault as the knife met her forearm and sliced clean through wool, silk, skin and muscle until it grated against bone.

Chloe screamed his name.

'Sam. Sam.'

Her foot lunged convulsively and caught Debbie on the hip, sending her sprawling.

Sam watched it all from the dazed perspective of a grief so deep it had numbed his senses almost to the point of catatonia. Jo had come for him, that was clear. He felt only an utter conviction that he would soon be with her, hold her, love her again. Somewhere in his mind the memory of a conversation drifted in and out of tune like a medium-wave pirate radio station.

195

'Has anyone . . . counselled . . . As much a victim . . . as your . . . wife . . .'

He saw Debbie with the knife, saw the blood spurting from Chloe's arm, saw her desperate retreat and it looked about as real to him as a Loony Tune.

And then the woman was screaming his name again, screaming in fear and terror. It broke through the cotton wool of his mind like unwelcome ice water on a sunbather's back.

'Sam. Sam.'

His eyes focused on Chloe scrambling backwards, on Debbie getting to her knees with that terrible look on her face, black with loathing. And odd, galvanising anger filled him. This was not a place for anyone else to die. It was his place, his time.

He lurched to his knees as Debbie began to move forward and Chloe could only stare in horror at the knife she held with its wicked point.

A yard from Chloe, as Debbie wound up for the final thrust, Sam caught her and pinioned her arms. She fought like a cat, kicking, biting, scratching with her red nails. Breathing hard, Sam carried her bodily and threw her across the room. She landed heavily, the breath whistling out of her as he turned to help Chloe.

Ripping open his sleeve, he bound her arm as Debbie slowly stood to face them. Chloe scanned Sam's face. He still had that off-kilter look in his eyes. A displaced look. It frightened her.

'It isn't her, Sam. It isn't Jo,' she pleaded.

Across the room, Debbie was watching. She picked up the doll and caressed it with the knife, smoothing away the hair from its face with the blade, speaking soothing words between sharp glances at Chloe.

'Maudie wanted her baby, Sam.' Debbie fixed Sam with a sideways glance, the doll's cheek pressed against hers.

Sam didn't look at her. His eyes pleaded with Chloe and it was heart-rending to see. 'The message,' he said.

'What about the message? It was Jo's voice on the tape. I know it was.'

'No,' pleaded Chloe. 'It wasn't. It couldn't have been.'

'It was. She wanted me to help her. *Help her.*'

The voice, when it spoke, took them both by surprise. Sam was looking at Chloe, his eyes blazing with angry insistence, when he heard it. He saw the horror in Chloe's eyes first before he swivelled round to look.

'Help me . . . help me . . .' It was plaintive, small, childlike, with an added mocking note. But a perfect rendition of the voice both he and Chloe had heard on the answerphone that dark Sunday evening.

It emerged from the grinning face of the woman rocking back and forth with the doll in her hands like a little girl pleased at being able to show off a party trick.

Sam began to tremble and shake his head.

'No, please, no . . .' he muttered.

Chloe squeezed his arm and spoke gently. 'Let her go, Sam. Let her go.'

For one hopeless moment, Chloe thought that Sam had fallen again into that dark pit. His eyes lost focus and his voice trembled into a low moan. He let go of her hand and walked slowly across to Debbie.

She smiled triumphantly, still rocking, the knife still working, scraping small plastic shavings from the doll's face.

Sam got within two feet of her before he spoke.

'You killed her.'

Debbie stopped, her face twisting in an insane mask of rage. The knife flew up in her hand, but Sam was ready, his feet balanced and muscles bunched. He caught her wrist easily and twisted. The knife fell, clattering.

With his other hand, Sam wrenched the doll roughly from Debbie's grip. She exhaled in shock, as if it was her very breath he had stolen.

'My baby,' said Sam. 'She was Jo's and mine and you killed them both.'

197

In front of him, Debbie's face crumpled into a wild grimace of anguish. Her teeth were bared, her neck muscles straining and taut as piano wire as a keening sob finally broke from her mouth.

Sam turned and said to Chloe: 'Call the police.'

At the door, he turned and looked at what had once been his wife's twin sister. He let his gaze fall to the plastic doll he was carrying. He stared at the battered replica of a young life and shook his head sadly before tossing the flaccid toy back across the room.

He stood at the grave-side, staring at the stone that bore her name.

Fresh cut flowers lay on the fine gravel beneath his feet. He had been there for almost an hour, talking to her, reminiscing. He had brought two wreaths as well, and had wept for his unborn child when he'd laid the smaller of the two. It had taken him almost seven months to do that.

It was a bright, windy day. He was alone in the cemetery. That was how he had wanted it this first time.

Behind him, in a yard hidden from his view, some schoolchildren were running and shouting on their way to meet mothers and fathers at the end of their day. Sam found it an oddly reassuring sound. The sound of life. The sound of the future. He smiled to himself and turned towards his car.

It was warm inside, the sun through the windscreen bright and low. He started the engine before he turned and smiled at her, the sun bouncing off her Viking hair.

'Feel better?' she asked, her shoulders hunched forward in that insecure way of hers.

He nodded. 'Sorry I was so long. I've really buggered up your afternoon. What is Mr Urquart going to say?' With that, he lifted up her chin. Her hair fell back from the sculpted smoothness of her face.

'Who?' asked Chloe.